Duty's Dad

Richard Watson III
1792 - 1849

K.G. WATSON

Dedication

To my daughter, Laura, for inspiring this project.

CONTENTS

1
RICHARD'S ACCIDENT

"Mother of Mercy," Susannah shrieked as the kitchen door slammed open behind her. Against the frame sagged her husband, Richard carrying a limp load. He caught a breath then staggered to the table cluttered with her meal preparations. She swept a space for him to lay his burden - his dust-caked and unconscious namesake.

The child's mouth was slack, his left arm dangled oddly. Richard was still breathless from running down the street carrying the child. Susannah's first-born breathed slowly but barely.

"Some scaffolding broke," Richard senior gasped. "I think he was hit by some falling stone."

Susannah snatched a kitchen cloth from a peg beside her, soaked it in the bucket of well water at the edge of the hearth in one motion and was at the table in two fast steps. She patted the blood running down the boy's face but more oozed from the hairline. She followed the trail up into his scalp to a 2-inch gouge on top of his head.

"Oh Richard," she whispered and clutched her husband's arm for support. She swallowed hard and took charge, "Get me some more water."

Richard squeezed her shoulder and turned to the cupboard for a bowl and back to the bucket.

"Here," he whispered setting the bowl beside his son's head.

Their child's face was as grey as the stone dust that covered it. Susannah wiped him cleaner, then her fingers carefully felt behind and along his neck. Nothing amiss!

"His arm doesn't look right," Susannah whispered as she wiggled it gently at the elbow.

"Dear God, he's broken some bones," groaned Richard.

"I'm not sure," said Susannah more firmly. "Go get the midwife. She'll know what to do. Hurry," Susannah directed.

Richard touched his son's face lightly before he dashed out so fast, he forgot to close the door. With clenched teeth and brimming eyes, Susannah reached beneath her apron now muddy and blood-streaked, for the mending scissors that swung on a tether from her belt. Susannah nipped out the stitches of the seam under junior's shirtsleeve.

"Please God. May he need it again," she thought.

Snip, snip, snip went every fifth stitch in far less time that it took to make them. Yank and yank again, the sleeve was open. No cuts on his arm.   With the same skill she opened the side seam of her son's shirt. The boy's arm flopped like the rag with which she had washed him. Peeling back the shirt she studied the band of purple and red bruises drawn broadly across his chest from left hip up to that ear.

"Oh Lord! How had this happened? Something had to have landed on him. A plank?" She wiped away the dust and listened to his shallow but steady breathing.

Midwife Murphy was at her elbow and nudging her aside. Susannah pressed into her husband who stood awkwardly behind, his hands on Susannah's shoulder.

"Lift the table towards the window," directed the stout woman. She grabbed one end and Richard and Susannah stumbled into each other as they fumbled to pick up the other.

As he passed close by the door, Richard kicked it shut against the eyes gathered outside. The midwife leaned forward over the boy. Her fingers slid with skill and long-knowing over the child's chest.

"Well if the ribs don't puncture his lungs, he'll keep breathing. This one, no, these two, are surely

3

broken," she announced with detached skill. "He's not going to like laughing for a while," and with a joke, threw Susannah a lifeline of hope for recovery.

"It's his collar-bone that broken. Kids this young don't usually break this bone or move it so much. Something really heavy must have hit him." She pressed the area tenderly, "I can't feel any splinters – seems like a pretty clean break. No skin broken. That's good. Hold him here."

The parents bumped clumsily as they stepped to the other side of the table. Susannah clamped down firmly on her son's other shoulder. Through the sleeve of her blouse, Susannah felt her husband's arms tighten to hold the boy's hip. Strong and old fingers pinched the end of Junior's collarbone through the skin and lifted as her other hand pushed and slid in one deft movement. It brought a long agonizing groan from the unconscious child and tear-stained cry from Susannah.

"If that arm can be tied tight to his body till the bone knits, we'll see how well he can use it later. It's his head I'm worried about." Mother Murphy had spotted the wet and parted hair that still oozed red. She pressed gently around the bleeding. "Block-headed as his Da', I'd say, but you'll just have to wait and see if he wakes up."

The midwife nipped off the corner of a square packet made from a folded dried leaf that she slid from her apron pocket and tapped some brownish powder into the clotting blood on the crown of Richard's head.

"Put a clean pad on top of that hurt and tie it on with a band under his chin. Change the dressing morning and night and wipe it clean only with well water and a clean cloth. Put a little of this on each time," she said as she gave Susannah the rest of the packet. "Keep him warm. I'd expect a fever over the next few days. Use a cool cloth on his head if that happens."

Mother Murphy stepped back a bit as she spoke and again with a critical eye scanned the child's un-torn pants and boots for blood. Susannah sagged into Richard and grasped for his hand. Richard bowed his head silently, his forehead touched Susannah's hair.

"If it doesn't show pus in two days, the skin should heal all right. But when he wakes up and how he'll be when he does, is in the hands of the Lord," concluded Mother Murphy.

Richard hastened to thank her and hold the door open. Susannah turned for some sheeting to bind the boy's arm. Two all-night vigils followed. A cot had been set up in the corner by the kitchen fireplace. Little more had been said about Junior's accident. Meals were made as usual. Richard had gone to work as usual. Junior slept fitfully groaning when his injured arm hit the side rail of the bed despite the blanket that padded it. Every candle stub in the house was burned, and the scrapings heaped about the last of the wick. There'd been almost no fever, but he still lay almost like dead.

It was in the gloom of pre-dawn on the third day that he woke drowsily and slurred "*Ma.*" In her chair at the bedside, she snapped alert, and was touching his face.

"My head hurts awful bad." He tried to raise his bound arm then looked at it in confusion.

"You took a heavy hit, son. I'll put a cool cloth on it."

In the three heartbeats it took to return to the bedside, his eyes were closed, but this time in sleep. Susannah pulled up his blanket and fussed to smooth his hair. Junior woke mid-morning still with a terrible headache he said, but he took a few spoonsful of gruel before drifting off to sleep again.

Susannah called Sarah, their 6-year old, in from the street where she was playing with the neighbour children, "Stay here and watch your brother while I draw some water. I'll be back as fast as I can. If anything changes, you come for me at the well like the devil himself is after you."

She swung the yoke from its peg at the door and picked up the rope handles of her two pails and strode down Mungret Street towards the well, two blocks down and one over. She walked fast despite the traffic. A dozen women called to her before she got to the pump asking after the child. Everyone knew.

"He woke this morning, Saints preserve him. I think he'll be alright," Susannah had called back daring to feel hopeful.

As she put her back into the long handle of the hand pump at the well, Mary MacNie, who was next in line, repeated the same question. There was no disguising the heart-felt sincerity of the question and the prayer in Susannah's answer.

"I saw it happen you know," Mary said with eyes on the puddles of splashed well water at her feet. I was peeling potatoes at the front door when I heard the shout."

"Richard said he was hit by something falling off the scaffold."

"Not quite."

Susannah stopped in mid-motion, "What do you mean?"

"Richard had the youngster working the few days before the accident, you know. Got O'Neil to have him fill the wall with the rubble. With the wall so high now, junior had to haul up the broken rocks in a hod. It had to weigh almost as much as he did. The mason working above missed the block tossed by his apprentice and it hit the ladder and knocked it off the scaffold when your lad was just about to the top. Fell 15 feet he did and landed on top of the ladder's side rail with the hod right on top of him. The hod's handle must've taken the weight before it broke otherwise your lad would've been squashed like a bug. I thought one of the broken rocks caught his head in the fall."

Susannah was as pleasant as she could be in thanking
Mary for her account as she scrunched her shawl into a
shoulder pad under the yoke and hooked up the pails to
it. But the news had hit her like the stone that the mason
missed.

*Junior was never going to be the horse of a man his
father was*, she said to herself. They'd talked about that.
How could Richard send their son to a task he couldn't
possibly do? She thought the boy had just gone to watch
and welcomed the feeling that Richard was showing
some interest in his boy. *What was he thinking?*

Susannah staggered home under the weight of the twin
pails swinging from ropes at the end of the yoke across
her shoulders. At one point, she felt so dizzy and faint,
she had to rest against the wall. *How could Richard do
this? Why? Why did he say it was an accident?*

Later, Susannah could not remember the events of that
afternoon. She must have spent them over the fire
finishing the stew; she found it bubbling gently when
Sarah returned and startled her by asking if she could
light a candle. Susannah found herself with the long
ladle in her hand stirring the iron pot mechanically. She
confused Sarah's voice, momentarily for young
Richard's.

Her eyes jerked to the child in the bed on her other side.
He still breathed but remained unconscious. As Sarah
touched the candle to the coals to light it, Susannah found
her mind wandering back to the pot and the ladle in her
hand, the prize of her trousseau - the days before her

wounded child was born.

When Susannah Farquar married Richard Watson, this large iron pot with two ladles had been a combined gift of both their families. The pot was cast iron - bulbous, and black by design and from daily use over the fire. It had a bale handle to hang on the fireplace crane. It had stout projections on each side of the rim for picking it up with two padded hands. It held a gallon easily and still had headroom, so it didn't boil over. The rim curved inward to direct splashes and drips back into the pot.

If the pot was big and stout, Susannah was not. She was small and wiry. Garbed in a belted, full skirt of dust-concealing grey and brown homespun topped by a long-sleeved dark blue blouse, she looked larger than she really was.

A full-length pale grey apron with a deep pocket on the right side protected her from splashes from chin to knee. Her ensemble set off almost-blond hair caught carefully into a large bun. The low fire before which she stood warmed an oval face right up to brown eyebrows. A sharp freckled nose separated brown eyes. An easy smile normally wrapped the whole package, but not today.

Susannah had set the ladle back in the bubbling pot and wiped her hands on her apron. She glanced at Sarah's placement of the candle on the table. The meat had not been the only thing stewing in the kitchen that long afternoon.

Susannah recalled every sentence of Mary's description

in her head. In her mind she saw her child throwing the waste stones into the V-shaped box till it was full enough to impress the foreman and his Da'.

She winced herself as she imagined him struggling to lift it onto his scrawny shoulder and how the box must have dug into the muscle along his neck. She could see him staggering to the ladder, lifting one foot then dragging the other up to it, tilting the box to miss the ladder rungs, slowly wobbling towards the top. In her mind she heard the shout, felt the falling, the crash, the jolt of pain and then darkness.

Susannah, again, found herself standing in the growing gloom suddenly not knowing what time it was and even confused about where she was. She couldn't recall what she was doing. She shook her head. What seemed like puzzle pieces slowly linked together. She checked Junior, still unmoving, in his cot by the fireplace.

Sarah had set the table. She'd been about to get the soda bread she'd made earlier out of the cupboard to go with the stew. That's what she'd been about to do.

The fire's glow and the single candle on the table lit the room when Richard walked slowly, bent shouldered through the door. At the trough down the street he'd washed off the stone dust from the Almshouse construction that he was overseeing. He stood a moment looking at young Richard in the cot then crossed to his place at the head of the table.

He lowered himself slowly into his chair. It creaked as he

leaned on its arms. His bowl and spoon were in place, a mug of small beer at the head of the bowl. The soda bread, a small bare board, and a pitcher of well water formed a triangle at Susannah's end of the table. The candle flame danced in the middle of the table. Without a word, Sarah climbed up on the cushion on her chair near her mother. It was dinnertime.

Susannah hoisted the pot of stew from the short 'S' hook that held the pot high above the coals and moved it to the bare board that protected her table. With a practiced hand she lifted two scoops of stew into the bowl that Richard extended towards her.

She handed it back then put a partial scoop into a bowl for Sarah and full scoop for herself before she said, "I heard from Mary O'Malley how Junior was injured," she said.

Richard's spoon stopped in mid-air. He looked up into his wife's fire-lit face as she levelled him with a look that was thunderstorm black. With eyes a-flicker, Susannah slowly rounded her end of the table like the fleet under full sail with every gun run out.

Stepping close to her husband and in a hiss that crackled, she whispered quietly and with thick fury, "I'll not raise sons for the likes of you to sacrifice on that altar of yours, Richard Watson. You can see he is not built like you and he'll never be the boss to bully or beat others into line. You know he shouldn't have been on that ladder. You knew that foreman of yours has something against Protestants and anyone but his kind! You handed him over to that sadist to toughen him up, didn't you? Well look what you have now! He might be an invalid for the rest of his life."

Richard had backed deep into his chair under her creeping approach. She was eye-to-eye and nose-to-nose with her husband.

"He'll work where he has a hope and that isn't on a ladder. He's going to school Richard Watson! And you'll pay and smile and don't you EVER let me hear a word of complaint or belittling him, or Richard Watson, I'll make your life a misery you can't imagine!"

In the next heartbeat the ladle in her hand smashed down on the table like the Hammer of God.

"He'll not be working with you again!"

Had his hand been on the table instead of the arm of his chair, Richard would never have used it again.

With the crash at the table, Junior jolted upright in bed screaming and looking about wildly in confusion with his arm bound securely to his side. Susannah was beside him in three steps. Behind her the scrape and slam she heard was Richard tipping over his chair as he jumped from it and banged out the door. Susannah held her son with her free hand till he settled. She asked him if he'd like some dinner then returned to the cupboard for another bowl and spoon, and to the pot for a small serving. With a swish of skirts, she strode to the cot to feed her son.

The dint made by Susannah's ladle slamming into the table to make her point, could not have been better placed had she planned it. It was just to Richard's right, a few inches from both edges at the corner. He couldn't cover it with his dinner bowl or plate and worse, every time he put his hands on the table to rise after the meal, one fingertip or the other found it.

With the passing years, as the tabletop was scoured pine-white with continual use, that dint only darkened as food oils and Richard's fingertip stained it daily. Nobody ever talked about how it got there; nor was another word ever said about the dint in the bowl of the ladle either.

*

Three months later, with his sling gone, but a weak left arm, Richard Watson (III). was enrolled at the Diocesan School for Boys near the Mungret Gate.

2
RICHARD'S EARLY SCHOOLING

The Reverend Mr. Jones was Richard's teacher at the
Diocesan School. He had the air of the entitled, learned
at his father's knee when the Bishop had summoned
Jones's father to Limerick from Westminster. The family
had come to resurrect the school that had been founded
on the estate of Sir William King in 1611. What had once
been as glittering ballroom had been converted into a
classroom for fifteen children in worn canvas and home
spun. They sat in a curve on 6 benches. They looked
like stakes in a garden.

The Jones's had done a good job at the Diocesan School.
Set in an almost rural setting, the school was healthily
away from the smells and smoke most of the students
lived under.   Set up with continuing financing from the
Church Of Ireland and supported by well-heeled alumni,
the school could attract teachers of scholarship and
children of aspiring families. Set on the road to Tralee,
the school had enough passing traffic to distract flagging
students, overwhelmed by their education.   It had been

the obvious choice of Richard's mother. It was close to home. Her own father in the bookselling business, had recommended it for its proximity and the buying habits of the teacher. It was not a good idea for Protestants like them to run the gauntlet of Catholic neighbourhoods to attend the Blue School at St. Mary's.

Susannah walked Richard, in his new black porkpie hat and reworked black coat of her own, to school on the first day. The school was just beyond where old Mungret Street cut through the city wall. Because it was the thoroughfare out of Limerick to Tralee, Mungret Street was broader than most streets and pretty-well maintained as a road. That meant often muddy! Muddy or dusty, it was a busy street, made more interesting by the houses and businesses along it.

Building walls came almost to the roadway leaving only a narrow path for pedestrians escaping wagons and riders. In a few places, above the height of carriages, dormers pushed out from the walls to add a window seat or cot space to a room above.

Richard noted them as rain shelters. Every eye on this road knew Richard because most went to the same church, shared the same market or the parents bought and sold to each other. As Susannah marched, she nodded to those she knew. Richard's ears sagged with the weight of his mother's running commentary of names and connections.

"Mrs. Jessop made those really warm blankets we have, you know. So tight they are. She's the best spinner

and weaver I know. You must order a year ahead to get
wool for a sweater or coat from her. She has a trick to
make the yarn shed the rain without smelling like a wet
sheep. Be sure you always greet her kindly."

"Morning, Mrs. McPherson. Saw your son in the
market last week. Working out well on the estate, is he?"
Susannah asked as she passed the woman sweeping her
front stoop.

"A handsome bridle that is Mr. Mehan. Made for the
mayor is it?" She joked as she passed the harness maker
and then to Richard, "His uncle is the tanner up near
Blacksmith Bennis." It was hard to keep up with a
mother on a mission.

Susannah had negotiated an arrangement with Mr. Jones
of the Diocesan School for Richard's education. The
deal was as focused as the funds she had to work with.
Richard would attend daily during the hours of daylight
and return home each night. Richard had already learned
his alphabet and could read better than most his age,
thanks to his Grand Da' Farquar's encouragement and
profession as a bookseller.

When called upon to read from a text that Mr. Jones had
selected, young Richard did so with ease. Thus, Richard
was dropped into a group already formed. That moment
was an anxious one as everyone turned to stare at him.

*

Their first writing lesson was about to begin. Mr. Jones

stood in his worn black robe like a half worn pencil at the front of the class. He tapped with his yardstick for attention. All eyes swiveled silently his way. The Master assumed a regal portrait pose; it looked absurd in tattered contrast to his academic gown. When all were attending, the Black Robe lifted a stack of wooden-framed slates from the table at hand and handed one to each child with the reverence reserved for the Sacrament on Sundays.

The frames were evenly notched about four finger widths apart on each side. Ruler markings penned into the wood showed the slate enclosed was about twelve by ten inches. The slate was smooth and cool to the touch on both sides. Richard's slate bore a scratched star in the wood at the corner.

From one of the two boxes left on the table, a collection of straight twigs appeared, cut from the hedge at the front door.

"Use the twig like a pen and show me how people should hold it correctly," the master demanded.

Nervous glances flitted sideways from face to face to see what others were doing. There was hasty shuffling of the stick to the right hand by one child to Richard's right. Fingers were scrutinized and manipulated by Mr. Jones.

"If I see anyone holding chalk like that, they'll earn a rap from my ruler," threatened the teacher.

Anxious glances flashed around. Nobody knew what they

should do. The twigs were collected back into the box and similar-sized flattened sticks of chalk were passed from the second box on the table. Richard recognized the same material that Blacksmith Bennis used in his shop to mark metal before it was fired. The chalk felt slippery and was jagged on the edges.

"Pick up your chalk this way," the teacher instructed. "Three fingers touching each other and on top of the chalk, thumb beneath. Violinists hold a bow this way."

Everyone traded puzzled looks as they hastened to obey and adjust to the strange feel of chalk between fingertips.

"That is how you will hold your chalk. When held in that manner, it will not squeak. I will have no squeaky chalk in my room," came the voice from On High. "Questions?" The master asked rhetorically.

Silence reigned. The boy across from Richard tried to write with his chalk on his hand then the bench and finally made a small 'X' in the corner of the slate.

"Now write the letter 'a' in the following fashion," and the Master turned to his large slate supported on a massive easel beside the table. His hand floated across his large slate on a whirlpool of air leaving a chalky trail. "Do that," he commanded.

Richard looked quickly to his slate to mimic the teacher's action. Most hands smeared a jerky damp circle across their cool slates. Richard's hand flew as though he was catching a fly. The chalk whispered the required letter. *Whack* went the master's ruler on the wooden rim of Jason's slate – just missing his fingers.

"Hold the chalk as I showed you."

More frantic glances darted from Jason to see how the others were holding theirs.

"Other hand there," instructed Mr. Jones to the child on the end whose name Richard didn't know. "Make those letters bigger. Bigger! Fill your slate." The Master was becoming vexed.

Mr. Jones was warming to his task and striding about the room looking over student shoulders. Richard was reminded of a crow flapping after scraps. And so, it went. A letter a day for the first week during the time they spend on writing. Then up to three letters a day. There was relentless practicing of past letters and joining each to the old letters in unpronounceable strings. Copying and correctness were virtues to be sought.

Those who could not or did not develop the flowing roll of rounded letters soon found themselves at the teacher's slate at the front of the room waving like departing cousins as they moved from the monstrous to the minute.

Peter, who could never figure out in which hand to hold his chalk, had a bad time trying to get past the jerky stuttering of his hand across the slate. He welcomed Richard's hand over his as he tried again and again to get the roll and rhythm right. As the letter strings got longer,

the letters had to get smaller to fit on the slates.
Eventually, the Master explained that the notches he had
cut in the wooden rims of their slates marked imaginary
lines across the slate upon which they were to write.
Capitals filled the space between those invisible lines,
lower case letter were to half-fill the space.
Practice. More, more, and more again.

"Now for flourishes," the Master said one day.
"Here's how to make an 'F' for an official document."

The variation had appeared magically at the end of his
chalk. The letter the children all knew had almost
disappeared in a thicket of squiggles and curlicues.

"With this flourish you convey sensitivity to go
with a text you might be writing," said Mr. Jones.

Richard was watching so hard his eyes almost sucked the
chalk from the slate. Creativity peeked through a crack
in conformity.

"Here's how you might do it in a Barrister's office
so nobody can read it at all," quipped Mr. Jones. But the
joke was lost in the passion to copy as directed.

Richard was proud to show off his skill to his mother on
a black-painted board he could take home from the
school. And when he did, she could only shake her head
in amazement at a spirit set free. Da' said little about the
chalk marks one way or the other. His hand seemed to
find the dint in the table just as he was drawing breath,
and then he usually shook his head and settled back

wordlessly. For Da', chalk lines meant where to cut wood and stone, chisel and hammer guides for perfect straights, corrections to the angles of the earth.

It was after dinner on a Friday night that Richard announced that on Monday, he would be starting to use a pen. Mother looked up with admiration. Da' sipped up the last of his fish soup, wiped the bottom of his bowl with his bread, rose and walked quietly out to the Pub.

Da' was gone when Richard sat down to breakfast on Monday morning but at his place, surrounded by a halo of light that could only have been in his mind, was a penny knife he'd never seen before. He looked at his Mother.

"Your Da' said you'd need it to sharpen your pen. He left it for you when he was off this morning."

A thrill of almost overwhelming intensity ran through him.

Da' did notice! Did listen! He was not ignored! he thought. He was not a disappointment to his father. In that moment he resolved to be a Master Penman as his father was a Master Builder.

The dark polished wood of the penny knife's solid handle felt warm in his hand. It filled his palm like a spell. With pinched fingers he levered open the blade concealed in the handle. The blade was a bit longer than his big finger; it glowed silver grey in the window-light. The back of the blade looked heavy, thick enough to mean business but not brute force. The back curved slightly to meet the sharp edge in a firm point. The edge was sharp enough to score his thumbnail when he drew the blade across as he had seen his mother do when she sharpened her knives.

"Careful," cautioned Susannah with a smile from her place at the table.

Richard noticed a small but sturdy cap at the end of the handle on one side of the hilt. With a thumbnail he could lever it up when the blade was open. When tipped up, the cap became a shallow socket that received the tip of his thumb. On the cap's other side, the movement pushed a pin down through the extended blade to secure it in place. When he pretended to carve, his thumb naturally found the socket. It made the blade solid in his hand, comfortable – a professional ready for duty.

"The blacksmith added that," Susannah said. "Most don't have that part, but he was concerned that the blade might close on your hand by accident."

There was that word again - the one that had sent him to school. *Are accidents the excuse of the careless or the forerunners of new beginnings?* he wondered

"Someday, maybe all folding knives will have something like that to keep them open, but for this one, Mr. Bennis came up with that idea. He wants to hear how it works for you," Susannah added as she rose from her chair.

Flip up, flip down. Blade close. Blade open. Flip. It was hypnotic the way the pin slid down through the blade and turned the foldable to the fixed.

"Either your Da' or I can show you how to keep it sharp with the steel and strop, later. Now off with you," said Susannah as she opened the door for her son.

Richard slid off his chair and stepped for the street then quickly turned back and scooped up his breakfast bread and sausage he'd forgotten to eat. Richard left for school that day as proud as the Lord of Limerick.

*

"What's this?" Asked Mr. Jones when Richard displayed his new penny knife.

Jones's finger tried to flick the cap at the hilt. Richard couldn't wait to show the answer to his mentor's question. Richard took back the knife and with a small flourish, he opened the blade and then flipped the lever to lock the blade in place.

"That's very clever," said the teacher with admiration, "Let me see that again."

With a skilled eye, the teacher studied the extended blade, tilted the knife to catch the light, tested the heft, approved of the size, ran the edge across his thumbnail to test the sharpness. He couldn't help but flip the lever again.

"Nice," he murmured as he handed it back to

Richard's anxious outstretched hand.

"Now let me show you how to sharpen this quill so that it draws a nice line. Cut yours at an angle like this. See how that opens up the hollow part of the quill and leaves you with a flat blunt tip? When you dip it in the ink, the hollow fills and it gives you a small reservoir that will last a few letters or words depending on how big you write. If you want a fine line, you shave off a bit on the side. See like this. Now you do it."

Mr. Jones handed Richard a fresh goose wing feather. Richard gripped the shaft of the feather near the tip. His blade sliced a beveled cut below his fingertip producing a clean edge and rewarding smile from Mr. Jones.

"Some of us split the tip lengthwise because it draws the ink down better," Jones said as he demonstrated. "But it makes the tip more subject to catching in the texture of the paper and so make blots. You'll have to learn to twist the quill in your fingertips so as your hand moves in those big circles you've mastered. Your hand should always be dragging the ink out of the quill. When you try to push the tip, it will flick the ink all over the place and you'll get to do it again so pull the quill through the curve and turn when you pause at the corners."

The practice began anew - writing text from books, writing conversations, writing lists of fruit in the orchard, names of neighbours, hymn verses, poetry, text from the newspaper. Gradually the feather became a friend in his fingers. Richard developed a copperplate script and learned to spell flawlessly. He regularly borrowed books from his grandfather Farquar's library and copied pages of text. When his Grand Da' admired his work, he told Richard there was another way to use his skill and described how printing created the books he sold.

*

Reverend Jones also saw that Richard learned his arithmetic till he could compute faster in his head than he could calculate on paper.

"What must one pay for three books each costing one shilling, thru'pence, ha'penny Master Watson?"

"Three shillings, ten pence, ha'penny sir", Richard could answer before the echo of the question had died in the room.

"How many yards in three miles?"

"Five thousand two hundred and eighty, sir."

"How many drams in a barrel?"

"Trick question sir! Drams measure weight. Barrels measure volume. To answer, you have to tell us what was in the barrel sir."

*

By fourteen, Richard could go on to university or to an apprenticeship. Susannah already had determined that destiny.

3

THE BLACKSMITH

Mungret Street ran somewhat west and somewhat south through the Irishtown section of Limerick. The prevailing wind dictated the geography of the businesses along the street. Furthest downwind, at the southwest end, was the square where the market was held and where the animals were slaughtered on those days. Across the street were the next smelliest businesses - the tanner, tallow maker and the blacksmith.

For the tanner, it was as close as he could get to the hides as they came off the dead animals – same for the business that rendered animal fat into tallow, then candles. For the blacksmith, it was as handy as possible for the horses bringing in produce from the fields out of town, to stop at his door for attention to their feet. Because the Blacksmith was where he was, the wheelwright was next door. The barrel maker was also hard by the builder of wheels. Could the brewery be far away?

For Richard, the buildings were conveniently arranged. When a pork-pie hat and wool coat wouldn't keep you dry, the open space of the square was the place to get really storm-soaked as you were walking to or from school. You could zig-zag your way between doorways and overhangs all along Mungret to the High Street and beyond to the school, but the market area was exposed. You needed a safe stop there.

The cluster of businesses opposite the square was a refuge on wet days, and an excuse to dally on others. The tannery was really a complex housing of family enterprises where various of the Dixon cousins turned the hides and fats from the abattoir into leather and parchment, soap and candles. The smells were enough to discourage anyone from all but the most compulsory of visits except when the scenting of the soap almost covered the stench of the soaking pits containing the hides in various stages of becoming leather.

The days when the workers were scraping down hides to make parchment with razor-sharp, blunt-tipped curved blades, were less smelly also. The workers would let Richard touch the scraps they'd trimmed from finished pieces of parchment or even vellum and promised him when he learned to write really well, they might give him a few pieces to practice on. But the blacksmith was a port in a storm any day, and it was to its open door, that Richard was attracted without fail.

Richard loved the blacksmith's shop. He loved the faintly sulphur smell of the smoke. He loved the darkness with the glowing eye of the forge halfway back in the shop. He loved the pounding rhythms of the smith's hammer.   That clang seemed to call him as strongly as Sunday's church bell.

"May I pump the bellows?" he asked of Mr. Bennis one day on his way home as he stepped around the horse droppings at the open door and into the half-light.

"A moment please," the begrimed smith said as he used his tongs to roll some work glowing yellow deep in the coals.

He pulled a strip of iron out, laid it on the horn of the anvil and with a flurry of focused strikes, flattened out the piece as the metal faded to dull red. Then back went the iron into the flames.

"Come over here and pump the bellows slowly for me," called Bennis.

Richard stepped closer to the heavy heat and personal space of the metal worker. For a few moments, Richard became the sorcerer's apprentice.

Whoosh! Whoosh! Richard worked the long handle of the bellows right-handed because it hurt to use his left as Bennis did. Air drove up through the coals in the forge turning the flames blue tipped as they caressed the dark work lying amidst them. *Whoosh! Whoosh! Whoosh!* The flames leapt with each pull. Gradually the iron changed from black to red again.

"Slowly," warned the smith. "You can do too much of a good thing. That metal is thinner now, so it heats up faster. Stop!" Richard's arm froze in mid motion.

The heat had spread from the edges turning the dark middle of the iron into a uniform yellow throughout. The smith poked the coals around the metal with his long tongs. When the metal's golden glow shone like treasure in the forge, tongs pulled it into the air where it bathed the shop in a flood of colour.

"Well done," Bennis said.

Bam, bam, bam, bam bam, bam. With a hail of hammering, the metal stretched round the curve of the anvil's horn and grew wider and thinner as well. The metal strip now looped well below the horn but because the horn was tapered, the metal band started to look like the lowest slice of a very tall cone. The cycle was repeated three more times before the ends of the band of black iron looped deeply below the anvil's horn and overlapped by three finger-widths.

With a flip of the tongs, the dull red band of metal was plunged into a half-barrel of water at the corner of the forge furthest from Richard. A phantom of steam rose from the tub. Another flip of the tongs and the cooled circle settled over a test barrel set on a stump beyond the water butt. It stopped just above a band already in place around the cask. The new ring sloped snugly against the bevel of the barrel staves.

"Hmmmm," muttered Bennis. "One more heat."
"Back off now," said the smith. "Let me handle this."
Richard stepped obediently to the end of the bench where
he could see but be out of the master's way. With a brush
of wire bristles that reached into the space between the
overlapping ends, Bennis polished the surfaces that
almost touched each other. Down from the shelf over the
bench he lifted a fist-sized pot and with a small slat of
thin wood, he lifted out some black powder.

"This is the magic stuff," whispered the smith
with a hasty glance towards the door for effect.

Showing almost feminine care, the smith filled the space
between the overlapping ends with the magic powder and
lovingly moved that part back to the forge. With his left
arm pulling slowly on the bellows handle, he coaxed the
heat up again, again, and a bit more. The metal passed
through red and was glowing yellow now. A spark
jumped from an end.

Richard almost missed the master's smooth lift of the
ring from the fire, the ballet step to his left that placed the
sparking metal on the anvil and the three blows of the
heavy hammer that sounded almost as one that welded
the overlapping ends of the band together. A grunt of
satisfaction escaped the smith as held it up to the light
from the door. Then it went hissing into the cooling water
again. Again, for effect, Bennis tossed the completed and
cold ring over the test barrel and it settled just above the
one already in place.

"It's too small," observed Richard.

"When I heat it up, it will be larger. It will slip down to the level of the one you see there, and we'll chill it in place. As it cools, it'll shrink and pull the staves together nice and tight – that is if the cooper makes his staves the same as those ones," he joked.

Richard didn't understand the quip.

"So, what was it you wanted Master Watson?" He asked, reminding Richard of his purpose.

"I came to thank you for the penny knife you made for me," Richard said with all the sincerity he could muster.

"You're most welcome, young man. How do you like the blade-fixing pin?" Bennis was obviously proud of his trick.

"It feels so solid and safe in my hand." Richard was fingering his knife in his pocket as he spoke. "I want to thank you for it, Mr. Bennis. But, me Ma' said to tell you she's had to reinforce the bottom of both pants pockets to be sure I don't lose it. It was wearing a hole."

"Glad to hear you like it. Don't you lose it young fellow! There's not another like it hereabouts."

"Mr. Jones, at the School, would like one as well," Richard offered.

"Well tell him to come along when he can. Oh!

And tell your Ma' I'll make her a metal pocket to put in your pants if she'd like," joked the blacksmith.
Richard wasn't sure what to say. A metal pocket didn't sound like a good idea to him.

To end the silence and get back to another barrel hoop, Bennis said, "Best be on your way. Your Ma' will be looking for you."

4

APPRENTICESHIP

"Richard is it?" asked the voice with a bit of an edge behind him. "That's not an Irishman's name, now. How come you're here?" The tone was accusing, confrontational.

Richard swiveled about on his tall stool from the workbench to acknowledge the challenge from what he thought was another apprentice in the Type Setting Room. Sean was struggling by with a tray of lead type headed for the workbench across the sun-bright room where the master printer was setting up the type for the first page of this week's Limerick Chronicle. The big smile belied the critical opening. It was to get his attention and it had.

"I'm Sean O'Connor. I heard the foreman call your name when you came in this morning. You're the new lad eh? Any relation to the boss?"

"Richard Watson," came the cautious reply with a

nod and, "Yes, but distantly. He's a cousin. My Ma' leaned on him to try me out because of the accident that hurt m-my shoulder."

"Well hoisting these trays is as hard as hoisting rocks but at least they don't fall on you from a great height."

Everyone seemed to know about his accident even after all these years.

"Talk later,'" whispered Sean as the broad back, tall shoulders and tow-headed curls responded to the shout that summoned them.

Richard returned to wiping the ink from his plate of type so the cleaned letters could be reset later. The coal oil fumes made his head spin, so he was glad of the chance to turn around for a few words and a few breaths of thinner, clearer air. It was also a relief to hear a cheerful word, even if it was a bit nosy in its intent. Oh well! No secrets on the street.

It was mid-day before Richard had another chance to chat with Sean over a small chunk of cheese and crust of sourdough bread. They were sitting in the sun on the back steps of the newspaper printing office under the second-floor windows of the Type-Setting Room.

Richard was studying his ink-stained, grey linen and wool shirt. The bib on his knee-length, canvas apron had protected the front of his shirt but not his cuffs and sleeves. Too late he'd decided to roll them up. He'd tried to take off the stain with the solvent he used on the letters but all he'd done was smear the blackness. There'd be the Devil to pay when his Ma' saw the mess. *Maybe I should ask for black shirts?* He wondered.

Sean broke into his thoughts, "So where's your name come from then?"

Richard paused before answering. It sounded like a sincere request, if a bit impertinent but he yearned for a friend, "Well if you must know, I got it from me Da', and he from his and that one got it from a martyr to the cause."

"So that makes you Richard The Third! I think I'll call you Your Majesty", Sean mocked with a smile, bow and flourish!

"Weisht," Richard said as he ducked a look around and up at the windows above them. "I'm not supposed to be dead on the job first day!"

It was not an idle anxiety. Catholics had recently beaten loose-lipped Protestants to death for similar slips.

"Martyrs are my territory," chuckled Sean. "St. Mary's is big on martyrs." Sean waved expansively, "We got 'em by the boxful you know. There aren't enough days in the year for 'em all. Me Ma' tells me I was named Sean because there isn't a saint by that name anywhere. And she reminds me every time she grabs me ear. You're no saint, says she," he continued, "but at least

I didn't have to die to be famous. I think she's not telling me the real reason though," he went on after a pause, "I've never knew me real Da. British soldier he was, I think. And she named me Irish just to spite him."
"So back to you," Sean asked, "Who was the first Richard – your Grand Da?"

"The old man was named in honour of the Regiment Patron where his father, John, enlisted. John enlisted because everyone his age signed up too. There was no hope staying back in Lanark County in Scotland in '24. John was a big, strong lad and they handed him a pike in the breath after he picked up the king's shilling. Done he was then. They were scrounging for recruits to make up the numbers before they shipped out to keep the peace here in Limerick."

"Army of occupation you mean," spat Sean. The bitterness of recent times came out together with memories of the old.

"Well, whatever! But it was the story of the Regiment's first battle that sealed the name of John's first-born son and tradition looked after the rest all the way to me."

"So, a big victory was it, that covered you in glory and killed your namesake?"

"Not likely! It was so close to catastrophe that I'm lucky to be here at all. John, my Great Grand Da' heard the story so often that I think it bent his thinking permanently."

Richard shifted on the wooden step to get a splinter out of his seat. Sean leaned forward a touch. He could feel it. A story as good as a summer day was coming.

"Dunkeld, in Scotland was where John's regiment fought first. He wasn't in the regiment then, but I think he had to memorize the story along with the Bible they carried, to stay in the corps. And because he did, so did every one of us since – just to stay in the family. The Regiment was twelve hundred strong when it was ordered to Dunkeld to face five thousand Catholic Highlanders, of the Catholic persuasion. Covenanters, my kin were. They had been hunted down like dogs or taxed to death for decades for not coming to church, or not swearing that the King was head of the Church. When Argyle got the chance to form a regiment to protect us, he did and named it after the hero who was executed because he led the previous revolt. Richard Cameron was his name and the Regiment was the Cameronians. So, with 6 months training, and just figuring out which end of a musket or pike to hold, they were ordered to face this army of Catholic Highlanders bearing down on Dunkeld. And that's where I got my name."

"So, it's Richard Dunkeld or Dunkeld Richard," joked Sean with a wrinkled brow and twinkling eye.

"No, Stupid! Just '*Richard*'," he said with a swipe that Sean ducked.

"So, how'd you make out against the Highlanders?"

"It did not go well for the Cameronians. Fortunately, the Jacobites, that's the Highlanders, you know, seem to have forgotten to bring ammunition or powder for the artillery. It's something they'd be expected to do you know," Richard added with a twisted smile.

Sean saw a thousand-yard stare slide over Richard's face as he stood with the warriors of that distant day.

"The fight quickly became house-to-house fighting as we fell back to one barricade after another. When the Jacobite sharpshooters went upstairs in the houses to pick off our men over their barricades, a bunch of us ran off looking like cowards but snuck back around to the houses, locked the doors and set the thatch afire."

Richard shook himself back to the steps he sat on, "I can't help think of them screaming and pounding on the door to get out as the place burned down with them in it. What does it feel like to burn alive?"

Sean's eyes plucked the words off Richard's lips. He shivered and waved Richard on.

"It was midafternoon when the remains of the Cameronians made their last stand in the laird's mansion. By then they had all but run out of musket balls. All the senior officers were dead – a Sergeant was in command. He ordered most of the men to give their muskets to those at the windows and run upstairs to the attic to break through the roof and pull the lead sheeting, inside. They ran it down to the kitchen where some others had stoked up a roaring fire to melt the lead into their molds. It was into a bucket of water and the fresh musket balls went back up the stairs to the firing line."

The boys shoved over to let the foreman stomp up the steps past them.

"Quickly," urged Sean.

"So, at a break in the firing, the sergeant ordered up all the leftover kitchen firewood to stack along the walls. If the Jacks charged, they'd shoot their last shots and then use the muskets as clubs and any swords they had left to defend the place. But the enemy would not take   this place. They would burn it down with the attackers and themselves inside first.

"Aye, what does it feel like to burn to death in a fire you started yourself?" Reflected Sean at the repeated thought.

The tale was broken up by shouts from the Setting Room above.
"Where are they? Who do they think they work for?"

The kids dashed up the steps back to their duties leaving the conversation to hang in the dusty sunlight. Richard went back to work cleaning off the inky type on the second frame that held the back page of last week's Chronicle. He blotted the excess ink off the lead letters locked into the printing frame by first spreading a soft kerosene-soaked cloth over the frame and brushing the cloth flat with a slightly stiff bristle brush. It pushed the cloth gently down between the letters. The letters were made of lead and soft enough to scratch with a fingernail, they had to be treated gently.

Once Richard had removed the bulk of the ink on the cloth, the bristle brush itself cleaned out the spaces between letters, the holes in the a's, and p's and d's, and spaces between the lines of print.

The brush bristles themselves were then wiped clean on another cloth. The final blot was with torn or scrap paper to lift out the last of the blackness and pat the plate dry. Then the wedges that held the blocks of letters in place were tapped out and the letters came free. Each letter had to be picked up, wiped again with a dry cloth, and put in its own box in the tray.

"God help you if you get them mixed up and in the wrong box," swore the foreman. "And worse yet if you don't put the oily rags and trash paper in that tub with the tight lid. You can burn the place down if you forget to do that. So, mind I never see oily rags lying about and that lid not jammed tight on the tub," the foreman continued with menace.

He stood back with a glower. "But if you need something to start the fire on a damp morning, a handful of rag works really well," he winked.

The job was interrupted when Richard was summoned to help offload paper supplies from a wagon that had just arrived at the loading dock. Soon enough he found he couldn't lift the bundles of paper. They were far too heavy. But once he admitted he could read and write; Richard was told to check the count in each bundle and write it down instead. Sean couldn't do that and the glint in Sean's swagger and claim to be '*Supervising Slave*' dimmed just a little.

It was dark when young Richard left by the back door of the print shop and rounded onto Mary Street heading home over the bridge. His eyes were so sore from the fumes, they felt square.

"So, what happened?" Sean jogged up beside him.

"Well, after we got all the paper in. I sorted all that type I cleaned this morning and cleaned up the workbench. Not fast enough for the foreman but at least I didn't have to do it by candlelight. How do the printers see those letters in the almost dark?"

"The army, stupid! What happened to the army? The Cameronians," Sean urged as he poked Richard's arm to remind him where their earlier conversation had stopped.

"Oh. Well it seems that the Highlanders had stopped firing because there was some argument in their ranks about how this wasn't the bargain they signed up for. They didn't think it was supposed to be so hard to whip a bunch of rank Lowlander recruits. It had cost them too many men so to hell with it, they said. They all decided they were going home and so they did."

"Hmmm," was all Sean could say.

"The best part of the story was that the Cameronians came out of the mansion shouting insults and scorn at the departing soldiers. I mean real scorn and ridicule. 'Can't you do better than that?' 'Cowards!' 'What's up your skirts ladies?' You know the sort of thing. As they skulked away with their tails between their legs, they never knew there wasn't a handful of gunpowder left in the whole Cameronian Regiment.

"Cheeky bastards," chuckled Sean. "I'd tell you the story of the Boyne," Sean continued as they reached the corner of John and Mungret St. "In your story, you won. But at the Boyne we didn't. Nobody talks about it here except after they've been a while at the pub, or on the twelfth of July."

5
MARYANNE

The bell over the door tinkled as he stepped into the Cobbler's shop. The Cobbler was busy punching a row of holes to sew a sole onto the boot beside him. While Richard waited respectfully, he glanced at the sheets of leather hanging from the rack behind the man, the new slippers on the counter, the box of wooden lasts in the corner. He could see names written on each wooden foot. Richard's glance turned from the distractions as the cobbler set down his punch and mallet and looked over bent spectacles at him.

"I'll be needing new boots," he said to Mr. Hopkins, the cobbler. A moment of assessment passed.

"You're young Watson from over on Mungret Street are you not?"

"Yes sir."

"And you're apprenticed at The Chronicle are you not?"

"Right again sir."

"Yes, well I 'd need to measure your foot. You've grown a bit since I saw you last, young man. Maryann, bring me my measuring board," he ordered to the young woman who was coming in from the kitchen behind the workroom.

Richard thought he'd seen the gingham dress with long sleeves and high neck behind the long apron on the street and at the market. He thought she attended his church also. *This must be his daughter*, he mused.

Maryanne handed the cobbler the smooth plank he asked for as her eyes flickered to Richard. Hopkins directed Richard to a bench beside the door.

"Sit down and take off your boot."

Richard was glad he'd worn his fresh socks with the holes darned as he wiggled his foot free. The back seam of the boot was split almost to the sole.

"Well I guess you do need something now that your feet have stopped growing," Hopkins said as he positioned Richard's right foot on the wooden board and started to draw around it with chalk.

"Do you wear extra socks in the winter, Master Watson?"

"Sometimes but lately there hasn't been enough room," sighed Richard.

"Well then I'll give you a bit of ease here," said Hopkins as he redrew the line. "Let's see the other foot now." And the chalk tickled Richard's foot as it ran around his instep.

"All right. Now what kind of boots are you after? Something serviceable, I'd guess. I'll suggest something that comes up over the anklebone. A full sewn-in tongue to keep out the mud from those deep puddles and with lots of opening room will serve you well, I think. You have a high arch I see, and you need that space to get your foot in easily. I can adjust the instep to make that arch comfortable. Four-eye laces I expect? You'll be good for ten years with boots like that if you keep them well looked after," smiled the cobbler.

Richard could only nod. He hadn't expected so many questions.

"How much will that be?" asked Richard anxiously and blanched at the price.

"Well that's what it is for the gentry, but I have a task for you that could reduce the price if you could do it for me," added Hopkins.

"What's the task?" Richard asked with a hesitation.

"I hear you do some fancy letter work at the newspaper. Show me your name with a few flourishes."

Richard picked up the chalk, sharpened it into a blunt

point by rubbing it on the stone threshold. He lifted the measuring board and being careful to miss his foot outlines, he wrote his initials in the space available.

"I have a few customers who've asked for their initials to be stamped or stitched into the tops of boot flashings and the like. But I need something to copy so maybe you could make me a set of letters for that purpose."

"Here's another board. Show me some letters about the size of my thumb."

"I can't do letters that small with this chalk," Richard said, eyeing the blunt point, "but I could make them that size with pen and ink. Would that do? You want capitals, I presume. Maybe I could make separate letters on parchment. They would stand up to use. You could trace the letters onto thinner paper by laying parchment on a window glass and the tracing paper on top. You can see through the paper then to the letter below. That way you keep your master letter and make as many copies as you need. You could mix them as a customer needs."

With each statement, Richard's imagination bounced to the next thought and he spoke faster and faster. It was the cobbler's turn to nod in confusion as the thoughts poured out of Richard like a fountain.

"Good idea, young lad! So, let's make a deal; you give me a pack of letters about that size," he said holding up his thumb, "and I'll give you the best boots you ever had for half price."

He knew that apprentices had no money, but he had already negotiated a price with Richard's father at church and knew his father would pay it. So, with a handshake, Richard sealed the deal, wondering what he'd have to do at home to get his parents to cover the cost.

"Come back next week," said Mr. Hopkins as Richard opened the door.

*

It was a wet day when Richard returned to the cobbler for his shoes and found Mr. Hopkins was absent. Richard brushed the beads of mist from his fisherman's sweater and knocked his pork-pie hat on this hip. Maryann, who'd come from the kitchen when the bell tinkled, said her father was in Englishtown delivering new shoes to a wealthy customer.

"You won't believe how many shoes that lady buys," Maryanne continued.

Though she was wearing a blouse primly buttoned to its embroidered collar and a floor length skirt, she sashayed to the counter provocatively and slowly pushed Richard's new boots towards him. The boots glowed with fresh oil and wax. The stitching stood out black against the dark brown leather. Brown leather laces had been partly threaded in the lower two holes.

"Your name is Maryanne?" Richard asked, as he

looked up from the boots. He seemed to have missed her overtures.

"Good memory, Master Watson."

"Everyone calls me Richard."

"Richard it is then," Maryanne replied with a smile and introduced herself. Richard seemed not to hear.

"Here are the letters your Da' asked for," Richard said as he fanned them out like a gambler.

He'd trimmed the scraps from the parchment makers on Mungret Street into a tidy deck. Maryanne picked out the *'M'* and looked carefully at it.

"It's almost like a *'W'*," blurted Richard. "I put more flourish in than he'll need but he can leave out lines he doesn't want," he added leaning forward and catching a whiff of perfumed soap. Maryanne smoothed her finger across the *'M'* and then some other letters and looked up with a slow smile crossing her face.

"Could you show me how to write?" she asked looking straight into his eyes.

"Of course," Richard replied, flustered and caught off guard. "But it might take a while," he added with an attempt at recovered aloofness. "What would your Da' say?"

"I don't want him to know," said Maryanne a bit

conspiratorially, her smile full-blown. "Could you keep that secret?"

"Hmmm," said Richard with a twinkle.

Maryanne thought she detected a warming of interest in her.

"When could you teach me?" Maryanne asked.

"Let's start now," said Richard snatching up a clean measuring board and chalk from the counter.

Again, he sharpened it by rubbing the chalk on the inside of the doorstep. He didn't notice that last week's sharpening mark was gone.

"Here's an *'a'* and a *'b'* and a *'c'*," he said as he drew the rounded script letters. He handed her another board and the chalk.

"No. Hold the chalk this way." He moved around behind her and reached around her shoulder to show her, "Now as you draw the letter swirl your hand."

He held his hand over hers and swung it over the board. Maryann, though she stood perfectly still, tingled at his touch. Richard realized suddenly he had never stood this close to any woman but his mother and that his palm was damp. He lifted his palm on his fingers to try to conceal his sweaty hand and guided hers through the letter again adding a vocal accompaniment to the movement.

"Uuuup and Oooover, then back and down." His breath tickled her neck. His voice made a delicious buzzing sound close to her ear.

Maryanne was blinking as fast as she could to keep ahead of the tears of pleasure and the prickling, she felt all over. A clatter from the kitchen made them start and put some space between themselves. Maryanne scooped the two boards from the counter, laid them face-to-face, and tucked them on a lower shelf as though she had dropped something.

"Ahh! You're here," said Mr. Hopkins at that moment, as he opened the shop door and the bell tinkled musically.

"I'm home, Mother," he announced to the kitchen. He shook the wetness from his cloak and hung it, then his top hat on the peg behind the door.

"Now let me show you your boots, Master Watson." Hopkins didn't even stop to trade his frock coat for his apron as reached for the boots on the counter.

"First, here are the letters you asked for," interrupted Richard. "Are they all right?" Richard asked anxiously.

Hopkins studied them as he separated each and laid them along the counter.

"I put in more flourish than you might need, but if you stick to the darker lines you can customize each person's letters," Richard offered as he pointed to the embellishment on the swirling *'F'*, *'M'*, and glanced up at the cobbler's eyes. Richard saved pointing out the especially attractive curves of the *'H'* for last.

As Hopkins returned Richard's steady gaze he said with a chuckle, "Lad you have a commercial heart," He liked this young man. "They are fine, just what I was looking for. Now try on these boots."

As he guided Richard to the bench, Hopkins was thinking, *this man's talent for sales is wasted in a back room at the print shop.* Richard sat down, shrugged off his soggy footwear and put on the dry socks he pulled from his pocket. The smell of oiled leather blew up to his nose as Richard slid first one foot then the other into the boots. He didn't know footwear could be this comfortable.

"They feel wonderful!" he laughed.

"Well, you need good boots and a good bed because you're in one or the other for the rest of your life," laughed the shoemaker. "Lace them up this way," The cobbler showed him.

Richard stood.

"Let me see you walk."

Richard took a few steps away and back.

"Hmmmm. I think that right one is a little loose.

Just take it off." Hopkins picked up a scrap of thick leather and carved off a broad, half-moon shaped wedge with a razor-sharp curved blade. He thinned the curved edge then took the boot from Richard.

"Oops," he exclaimed, "I'd better take this off before the missus sees me working in my Sunday clothes."

His frock coat was quickly hung on a second peg behind the door. He picked up his heavy, scarred and stained apron from the nail beside the peg and tied it behind his back and rolled up his sleeves.

From the back of the workbench he retrieved a pot from which a stout, flat stick and a pungent smell projected. He stirred the contents of the pot with the stick before extracted a gooey, yellowish glob that he daubed and spread onto the back of the leather wedge evenly and almost to the edge.

With care, the wedge was then worked into the back of the boot's heel without daubing glue elsewhere inside the shoe. Richard watched as the shoemaker's strong fingers pressed the wedge firmly into place. The thinnest sliver of light reflected from the glue that oozed under the pressure to be exactly even with the top of the insert.

Setting the boot on the counter Mr. Hopkins said, "Let me show you how to look after these boots. This is for taking off the mud each night," he said as he handed Richard a brush with short stout bristles from a box on a shelf. "And then you rub this oil into the leather especially around the sole to keep out the water. Really work it in around the stitching if you want dry feet."

A can with a screw cap was plucked from the shelf beside the brush box. Then turning to a display case of clay pots, Hopkins selected one and continued.

"You polish them with this on a rag," he said as he passed him the pot with a waxy brown paste inside.

Looking about as though he had just recalled, the cobbler snatched a white cloth from a pile neatly folded on the display case shelf. Each item left Richard scrambling to accept it while trying not to drop the armload he had.

"You look after those boots young Watson and they will look after you. Because that glue needs to dry, you can't wear them till tomorrow."

"I'll come back after work then? Is that alright?"

As the shoemaker was agreeing, Richard thought, *and another writing lesson for … Maryanne or Maryellen. Maryanne…?*

"Good! Do that!"

While the men had been busy over the boots, Maryanne had started drawing her finger lightly over the letters spread on the counter. She looked over at the young man being fussed over by her father and she knew as surely as she was standing there, that Richard Watson was the man she would marry. Neither the baker's son with the wandering hands nor the leather maker's son who smelled like a wet horse, could possibly measure up.

6
THE READING LESSON

Richard Watson was approaching the end of his apprenticeship as a printer in 1814. He had only a few months to fulfill the time commitment, but he had already completed all the tasks and tests required of him to be welcomed into the Guild as a Master. He was twenty-two years old.

The secret of teaching Maryanne to write had finally gotten out when she surprised her father by writing out a bill one day. Since then, the excuse to get together had become Richard's teaching her to read. As Maryann's skill grew, he wasn't sure if he was happy or depressed at her rate of progress. How would they get together if she could read as well as he? In the couple years they had known each other, Richard and Maryanne had developed a companionable relationship and competition in poetic rhymes. Each tried to have something to offer at their next meeting and the competitive effort led to mutual appreciation of intelligent ability.

Richard had arrived for their regular reading lesson. He greeted Mrs. Farqhar as he entered the kitchen behind the shop and proceeded to help Maryanne move the table a bit closer towards the open door and window that led out to the garden behind the house. The light was better closer to the door.

The table moving had become a part of the ritual of their lessons. Richard wondered if Maryann's neckline was a bit lower than usual as they lifted the table. As they bent further to move opposite ends of the heavy bench up to the table facing the window Richard admired a beautiful flash of white skin below the Celtic embroidery on the neckline of Maryanne 's blouse.

Richard said, "You go first."

Maryanne struck a pose and in honour of her Scottish heritage held forth: 'A lively young damsel named Menzies Inquired: "Do you know what this thenzies?" Her aunt, with a gasp, replied: "It's a wasp, and you're holding the end where the stenzies".'

Mrs. Farquar chuckled as she took her rocking chair outside for better light and settled down. A dark wool sweater for her husband was on the needles. Knitting the cable pattern she had chosen needed all the light she could get to avoid a mistake. She also liked to listen to the couple reading and of course she was the couple's chaperone. Mr. Farquar was out with the men for the evening.

"Now yours," invited Maryanne as she sat down

and bumped her hip gently against Richard's on the bench.

Richard turned towards Maryanne and was rewarded with another peek down the front of her blouse as she turned toward him.

"There was an old man with a beard who said, it's just how I feared! Two owls and a hen, four larks and a wren have all built their nests in my beard."

"You'll have to keep yours trimmed so that doesn't happen," commented Maryann. "Now what have you brought tonight?"

Richard opened a small book of Robert Burns poetry that they had started last time but not finished. He turned to the last work.

"It's called, 'A Man's a Man for All That'," Richard announced as he tipped the book up a bit.

"Oh, you'll learn how to say it properly eventually," chided Maryanne as she made "All" into "Ahhh."

"Is there for honest Poverty That hings his head, an' a' that," Richard began

Maryanne leaned forward as Richard murdered the pronunciation, to look at what he was reading. Her firm breast stretched the fabric of her blouse as it rested lightly on the back of Richard's arm. The movement opened an even larger pucker in her scooped neckline. A definite push on his arm as she straightened to recite the lines as her parents would, made Richard squirm at the casual intimacy. Together, each gently correcting the other, they read their way to the bottom of the page.

"…That Man to Man, the world o'er, shall brothers be for a' that."

"Do you believe that?" Maryanne asked Richard.

"Yes!" he said. "If I never see another slur or abuse, I'll have seen enough Catholic - Protestant brutality to last a lifetime. We are all brothers and should behave as such."

Maryanne was a bit surprised by the vigour of the response and in the silence that followed it she shifted so that her leg pressed against Richard's again. He had to wiggle again to find room in his pants for the swelling that continued to grow. But he didn't back away from the firm leg that pressed through the thin skirt against his leg.

"How did you spend your day?" Richard asked sincerely.

"Oh, it was water-carrying day today. Eight buckets I had to carry, to fill the barrel in the kitchen. That was a lot. But it gave me a chance to catch up on the gossip at the well."

It was the same well Richard's family used near St. John's Square.

"And what is new?"

"Well, …" Maryanne seemed to be deciding what to say first.

The clicking of Mrs. Farquar's knitting needles had been replaced by a rhythmic breathing. It seemed the sound that made up her mind.

"Well … Do you know Jenny?" Maryanne whispered.

"Generous Jenny?" confirmed Richard, catching himself to match her whisper? "The one of Generous…. Proportions?"

"Yes, that's her. Well she had the juiciest bits to talk about to-day."

"I thought you just talked about the weather," smirked Richard.

With a throaty chuckle Maryanne turned slightly, "Jenny was telling us all about her Catechism lessons she's taking at the Cathedral."

"That must have been riveting," groaned Richard quietly with a lifted eyebrow that went askew when he felt Maryann's hand sliding touching his thigh.

"She was telling about what happened after the classes - after they completed learning about the ways we come to know God."

Richard was becoming aroused as Maryann's hand kept advancing slowly.

"This sounds like it was interesting." Richard was whispering. "But what did the priest have to say?"

"Well who did you think was leading things, Dummy?"

"Let me show you what Jenny was telling us," Maryanne said.

In the semidarkness, Maryanne gave a graphic demonstration that left Richard gasping.

"For the whole package, Richard Watson, you'll need to put a ring on my finger," she whispered slowly as she held up her splayed fingers. Then she stood straight and shrugged back into her blouse.

"Is that all Jenny told you about?" Richard whispered hoarsely.

 Maryanne chuckled.

The day after he was made a Master Printer in the ceremony at The Guild Hall, he asked for Maryanne 's hand.

They continued their reading lessons with increasing interest in new authors and styles and were married Feb 29, 1816 in St. John's Church of the Church of Ireland, down the street.

7

JOINING THE MASONS

Richard Watson's apprenticeship as a printer at the Limerick Chronicle lasted seven years. During a time when most young people make many lifelong friends among their workmates, Richard Watson didn't. He had lived at home rather than in a bed in a back corner of the shop and thus escaped some of the abuses that the two others like him suffered at the Printing Office. He was related to the owner. That was another reason for not being part of the true labour force. And of course, he was a Protestant in a labour force that was mostly Roman Catholic. It all meant he was an outsider to them. His skills also set him apart adding yet another reason for fellow apprentices to shun him. Having a single Catholic friend, one would stand up for him was the last straw.

By the time he was called to the Guild Hall to be acknowledged as a Master Printer, he had put some weight on the thin frame he inherited from his mother, but any place his shadow fell, it could still be covered by his father's. He was as strong as his fellow apprentices, except in his left arm, but he never got into the contests of who could lift the biggest bundle of paper. It wasn't that the other apprentices were hostile. They simply didn't offer back the help that he offered them when they were sick. They didn't return the extra work he took on to blunt the point of some punishment they'd received. The crass jokes and anal humour were not shared when he came by.

Richard usually understood instruction on the first explanation and only made the others look bad because of it. He was figuring out efficiencies in a task while they were still learning to do it. He found he didn't fit into the competition for being the slowest to learn.

"You can't put that much ink on the pad in this weather. The moisture in the paper makes the ink bleed. You must put a little ink on each time and do it more often," came the echo of the foreman's exasperation from a distant day. "All these pages have to be thrown out. Do it now," he thundered at the unfortunate apprentices, "and wipe the printing pad clean before you re-ink and start up again!"

Richard learned the skill of hand typesetting with a speed that surprised his journeymen overseers and his success doomed him to a monotony that the Master Printers could not imagine. The steps of passage through the apprenticeship were well marked and rigidly enforced. Most trainees required the repetition in which the procedure reveled. Richard did not. His work was refused more than once, without being proofed, just out of perversity. He could not, at his level, have already mastered setting type without spelling errors, or backwards letters. He should not be able to sort letters back into the trays for reuse so quickly. His fellows thought he was always cheating. They just hadn't figured out how.

The skill that saved his sanity was his penmanship. Because he could write so well, he was regularly required to draw up wedding invitations, visiting cards and letterheads for stationery. He got to be good enough to be involved in making the engravings for this profitable offshoot of the newspaper business. His sure hand graduated from resting on a bridge above the waxed metal plate to free-hand guidance of the pointed stylus that sliced through the wax. With all the flourishes, Richard would have made his teacher, proud.

As soon as Andrew Watson, the newspaper's part-owner discovered how much money Richard's work made for him, the word was passed for Richard to be reassigned to these jobs rather than the mundane tasks of the other apprentices. Another nail was pounded into Richard's social coffin.

Because he was regularly involved in the highest quality printing jobs, Richard had to learn more about the kinds and qualities of paper than an ordinary newspaper printer. Nobody else at the Print Shop cared or was interested – except for Sean O'Connor. Sean soaked up Richard's discoveries like a mop does water. To Sean, Richard was telling stories of an exotic world about which Sean could only fantasize. Richard spun out how he was following the evolution of inks and colours that printers used. The gleanings of Richard's chats with the Engravers suppliers where Richard had been sent to pick up materials for visiting cards, and writing paper for the carriage trade, was forbidden fruit to Sean. By age twenty and in the time many took to lift a bundle of paper, Richard could have rubbed a page between his fingers and decided its cost per sheet based on its linen and rag content, thickness, watermark, durability, ability to hold or bleed ink, embossing qualities and transport costs. Because he had learned to straddle isolated disciplines with confidence, he was an unusual man.

Richard linked these daily discoveries to what he learned casually from his Grandfather Farquar. He never stopped *"spinning castles from thin air"*, as Sean used to say. With the printing of books and pamphlets commissioned by his grandfather Farqhar, Richard had brought yet another new stream of revenue into the newspaper office. While Richard was aware that his usefulness was being exploited, he really didn't seem to care enough as far as Sean was concerned. Richard's treasury was information he told Sean more than once, and that was something Sean just didn't understand.

*

"Don't you know he's growing rich on your back, Richard?" Sean said one day in exasperation. "It's obscene how fat you're making that cat."

Sean had fallen in beside him as they both walked home after work.

Richard only shrugged, "You know, Sean, when I have something like the puzzle of matching papers and inks, letters and fonts, customers and schedule to think on and the possibility of making something outstanding, I don't smell the corpses hanging on the bridge so much."

His eyes flicked rightwards to see if anyone else had been added today to the streetlight standards over the bridge downstream.

"It's a place I can go while my fingers set the type that lists those who got how many lashes this week or were deported to the Colonies. I..." His voice trailed off as he rubbed the heel on one hand on the other. "The legal system seems run by sadists, but don't you ever lay those words at my door," he mumbled as he turned to look at Sean.

Sean wasn't sure what the word meant but it sounded vicious enough. They paused, as was their custom, at the corner of John and Mungret Streets before taking their leave.

"What do you do after supper?" Sean asked honestly, "You're not much for the Pub life as I've observed."

"Well we like to read to each other, and my parents like to hear us."

"I didn't think you'd get to that stage so quickly," jested Sean. Richard just smiled.

"And you?"

"Well I'd like to look in on Jenny tonight," said Sean hitching up his belt. "You know her, don't you?"

"Jenny the …Yes! I've heard she's quite…popular lately."

"Well another slice isn't missed from a cut loaf, is it," chuckled Sean. "You should …"

Richard turned and waved a silent goodnight over his shoulder.

*

Following their marriage, Richard and Maryanne came to live with Richard's parents in their house in Mungret Street. The couple took over Richard's room and that made the space as cramped as newlyweds should expect. It was a wonderful match. Susannah, Richard's mother, treasured Maryanne if only because she could reach down things in tall cupboards and do some of the heavy work that left Susannah aching for days.

Susannah loved to listen to the Scottish songs Maryanne would sing as they worked. Richard's sister, Sarah, was thrilled to have a new big sister at least for the brief time before she married herself. And the new arrangement was only a 10-minute walk to Maryann's parent's house so Maryanne could visit them daily for mundane or contrived reasons.

Bedtime brought new pleasures to the couple as they explored intimacies about which they could not talk publicly. But comfortable crowding for two would be strained by three or four. In plain language, Maryanne felt there was no room in their bedroom for a child however much longed for by the prospective grandparents. That was the public reason. In private, and never talked about except with Richard, Maryanne feared pregnancy.

"It could be the death of me," Maryanne lamented.

Richard could only agree but chose to hold her close instead.

"And besides," she said, "not having babies seems much more fun!"

So, the newlyweds enjoyed themselves mightily in discovering many manners that did not produce a child.

*

Richard was a bit puzzled one day when his father asked if he'd accompany him that night to the local Masonic Hall. Richard had always thought the Masons were a trade club and was surprised when they entered that night to find Andrew Watson, his boss at the newspaper, Mr. Jones his old teacher, and Blacksmith John Bennis, all greeted him.

In the course of the evening he felt his eyes were opened, despite the candle smoke and hazy golden lamplight. At first, the event seemed to have a comic quality. There must have been fifty men all bedecked in sashes, spreads of medallions or chains of office. All had embroidered aprons that stretched over or under paunches of various sizes. He was the only person who seemed to think the grandeur might be a bit much. His father's circuit of the room before the rituals began, had him shaking hands with some of the most notable members of the community. That caused him to think again.

When the rituals that were open to the public started, Richard was ushered into a place to one side at the front, while behind, in ascending ranks of pews, the members stood and replied with one voice, the necessary responses. The bitterness found just beyond the front door, was replaced with a sanctity of spirit. Richard was impressed!

In explanation as they walked home, Richard Senior said that he had managed to get around some very sticky problems that beset his building business because of the contacts he made there.

"What the English have done to Ireland is as wrong as it can be, but short of Heaven, I'm not going to see that change. Yet in that building, we're all just men celebrating our commonality not our differences; we will never get enough of that. I can talk to people there I can't wave to on the street for fear of offending one of the entitled. I think that is an association you might appreciate, and it is why I invited you tonight. If you want to follow me into this Brotherhood, I know they will welcome you. It's a worldwide Community. Your membership would stand you in good stead anywhere."

"What does it involve?" asked Junior.

"Well there is a course of education to learn the rites. We meet weekly. There are high points in the year that demand extra service and you will grow in influence and personal satisfaction as you put the principals of Freemasonry into practice. You contribute financially what you can and the respect anyone earns is not measured by those donations."

"Can I try it out for a while?"

"Yes. But after a few weeks, you must commit or back away. It's not for everyone, and nobody will think ill of you for deciding not to join. You could always change your mind later even if you can't see yourself in this band of men at present. Are you interested?"

"I would like to try that, Da'," Richard said quietly.

"I'll tell the Secretary," Da' said.

In bed that night, Richard announced to Maryanne his decision to try out the Freemasons.

"Isn't that just like the United Irishmen or the Orangemen or any of those other excuses for violence wrapped up in brotherly bigotry? Beating up their neighbours and such?"

"Not from what I saw tonight," he replied, "but

I'm only committed for another couple weeks to find out more before I put my name foreword or not."

"Be careful," Maryanne murmured as she reached over to slide a hand across his bare chest

"I think you'd better take your own advice, madam; you don't know what you might be getting into,"

"Well, surprise me," she invited.

*

It was more than surprising at Christmas time in 1817, for the patriarch of the family to not join in the festivities as he had in the past.

"He was not feeling well," was what Susannah said, but from her wrinkled brow everyone could tell she had concerns she didn't voice.

The coughing started in the New Year - breathless fits of coughing.

"He doesn't cough up blood, you know," was what everyone said.

"That's a kindness," was what people replied.

Everyone knew there were illnesses just as fatal. Two hundred years later, doctors would call his illness, pneumonia. Richard died on January 16, 1818, not knowing that term, just that he could barely breathe.

The Freemasons liked to hold their memorial within the sanctity of their own hall. Speeches were made and praise given for a loyal and true Mason. When it was over, young Richard, who had become an initiate, was invited to take the place his father had always occupied in the pew. When he did, there was prolonged and supportive applause.

*

Sarah's wedding to Michael Cleary had to be postponed because of the funeral. The widow's weeds on the Bride's mother were not worn well at a wedding. When Susannah declared that Sarah should marry in the summer and that she would relinquish her mourning garments after only six months, she was breaking a big tradition. Sarah and John were married at the end of June, and Sarah went to live in a small house that Michael had rented across Mungret Street and closer to John St.

Susannah, in the week after the funeral, made a proposal to Richard and Maryanne, "I'd like you to help me trade bedrooms with you. You will take the larger master suite, and I the room with the single bed."

There were the usual protestations that she held place of honour, but she insisted on relinquishing it.

"It is too hard to warm a large bed alone," she said sadly. In renewed strength, she continued, looking at them both, "You are the master and mistress of the house now. You should have the space that goes with it."

Maybe it was that declaration. Maybe it was the spacious master bedroom. But Maryanne felt that an unseen balance had tipped.

They were laying side-by-side in bed looking into the darkness of the ceiling when Maryanne whispered, "Let's make a baby tonight."

Richard rolled to look towards her and asked, "What kind would you like m'lady?"

"I'd like to bear you a son," she said.

"Well, I guess that means we have to do it on that side of the bed," chuckled Richard.

*

Richard and Maryanne were diligent in their pursuit of a male heir, so it was no surprise to either when Maryanne said she'd forgo her porridge for breakfast and take only tea instead. She might as well have raised a flag when she made her preference known to Susannah. The women's eyes clicked, their cups touched in silent toast and the tea stayed down.

"Will you help me let out my summer skirts?" Maryanne asked, as she set down her teacup.

"I would be delighted," replied Susannah with a smile that lit up the room. "Maybe you could wait a while before you buy material for new blouses. You'll need larger ones I expect. Once you go fabric shopping, you might as well get Richard to proclaim your condition in a headline at the paper."

The thought made them both laugh.

"Well with that smile, you might as well announce me to the whole street from the front step, this morning," grinned Maryanne.

"I'll wear a sack over my head every time I go out," Susannah replied, and they both laughed so hard they could hardly catch their breath.

*

Nine months after they took over the master bedroom suite, Richard III and Maryanne Watson (née Hopkins), celebrated the safe birth of a son. He was named John Watson reversing a naming pattern of a century but reviving the family's Scottish ancestor.

8
I HAVE NO IDEA

Richard had to stand a round of drinks for the neighbourhood men at Fosbery's Pub the night of Oct 26, 1818, the night of the birth of his first-born. Te babe had arrived in the morning after an all-night labour attended by his mother and midwife Murphy who had probably birthed everyone Richard's age on the street. Richard had been able to buy drinks for others and conceal his small consumption, a condition he didn't like to advertise.

All the post-birth signs had been positive. Baby had a lusty set of lungs, Mom and babe had figured out the food supply chain, and both were snoozing quietly when he left the house after dinner. It was a haggard face Richard wore three weeks later when he made his way to the Masons Hall for the regular meeting. Again, he'd been congratulated, but this time, he'd been offered drinks at the bar after the ceremony and instruction. Again, he had to find a way to politely decline, or share these well-meaning offers of paternity because, as he was careful to admit, he just didn't like the stuff. An early experiment in drunkenness had led to such a shaky hand for days after, that he couldn't do the engraving he was expected to complete.

"I never knew I could be so tired," complained Richard to some of the elders about him at the bar. "The child wakes at all hours and loudly proclaims his demands."

''Fear not. It will get better," agreed the older parents with assurances that it was a passing thing and launched into loud laughter and reminiscences that lasted the rest of the evening.

While both Maryanne and Susannah tended to feeding, bathing, and clothing the baby, they both still encouraged Richard to hold and rock the baby after nursing or to burp him.

"It's the very chair in which I rocked you," observed Susannah as she handed young John, bundled in a blanket to Richard as he sat in the kitchen rocking chair.

Richard learned quickly that excited and energetic jostling of the cheerful child was not a good idea right after the baby was fed. Richard found himself mystified at his own fascination with the child's face. He stared at the child endlessly as he rocked him wondering how the women came up with the comparisons that left him confused.

"He cries like you did when you were a bairn,

Richard," said Susannah.

"Don't you think he has the Hopkins hands?" asked Maryanne.

"I can see Grandfather Farquar in his eyes."

"With hair like that, he has to be a Watson."

How did they remember all those things? Wondered Richard but his thoughts quickly turned to his conversation with Sean O'Connor earlier in the day.

The mail that brought the newspapers from London to the office of the Limerick Chronicle carried an ominous hint that niggled at Richard. The paper he was reading for articles to put in their own newspaper had been printed on a steam-powered press.

"How does that work," asked Sean O'Connor one day as they sat on their favourite step on the stairs leading down from the type setting room.

"Well a big boiler full of water is fired up till it shoots a jet of steam against something like a paddlewheel that is enclosed in a box. The paddlewheel is mounted on a long shaft that sticks out of the box. So, the paddlewheel turns, and it spins the shaft. Along the shaft are pulleys on which belts are mounted to take the power to the press and anything else that needs it. A spinning drum snatches paper from a pile, slips it under the press just as the type comes down. God help you if you have your hand in the way."

Sean reflexively rubbed one had with the other as he imagined the stamping action.

"The press I just told you about turns out a thousand pages an hour!" stated Richard. "How many does your team print in an hour?"

"We've never hit five hundred that I know of," Sean replied.

"Do you see where this goes?" Richard responded leading Sean gently to the obvious. Sean's mouth started to open, and his eyes widen.

Richard interrupted Sean's epithet with worse news, "Well that was the way it was four years ago. This article from London says the new press runs at FOUR thousand pages an hour!"

Sean was stunned! "So, either Mr. Watson, your cousin, won't be needing as many of us or to work as long to get out the newspaper," Sean commented acidly.

"When, this comes to Limerick," said Richard ruefully as he waved the newspaper in his hand, "Mr. Watson, my cousin won't be needing as many printers like me either. Steam is already making paupers of the spinners and weavers in town. My brother-in-law says he can bring in wool fabric from England cheaper than he can get fleeces processed here. So, what does he say to Mrs. Jessop down the street who has woven the best cloth any of us knows, for a generation? Yes Mrs. Jessop, we'll

take your wares but only at half last year's price? I think
not!"

Sean came rapidly to a boil, "Dump the machines
in the River Shannon, say I."

"Too late, Sean. It's already the law that we folk
can be imprisoned or sent to the colonies for damaging
those looms and the like."

"Well we refuse to buy steam-made fabric," shot
back Sean with a glare.

"Sean if you find you're only paid part wages,
what are you going to do to clothe, let alone feed, your
family?"

*

It was Summer in Limerick. John, Richard's first-born,
had been walking around furniture and eyeing the spaces
between with an infant's intensity. To get to distant
objects, he was regularly dropping to his knees and
crawling across the separating spaces. Such mobility had
inspired Susannah to show Maryanne how to tip the
heavy benches they used at the table, onto their sides to
first box off close approach to the hearth, and later to
fence John into a corner. They didn't want to find him
underfoot while they were preparing meals. There was a
risk of him being burned or scalded. Tethering worked
well for playing on the porch, but not as well inside
where John tangled up as fast as a puppy.

Richard and Maryanne had moved their armchairs to the

narrow porch outside the back door and John was marching around Maryanne's chair as though he had miles to go. He got to the nearest point to Richard's chair and stood looking across the space. With no warning, he let go of his mother's skirt and took one step towards the other chair. He was now wobbling on his own feet then took another step and caught one of the spindles supporting the arm of Richard's chair. Richard had just happened to glance down at John when he was in mid motion. A warning to the child caught in his throat. Maryanne followed his eyes to see the second step. She squealed with delight and a shout to Susannah to come and see. Richard smiled and said something silly as the moment's joy blew away the conversation that had churned inside him. It was some weeks before the novelty of John's walking wore off, but the afterglow remained. Again, they were sitting on the porch in the back yard.

"He's growing so fast," Maryanne was saying, "He'll be chasing the chickens soon."

"I wanted to talk about that," said Richard.

For weeks he'd been rehearsing how he would raise the topic and now that it was at hand, he forgot completely what he had prepared.

Instead he simply blurted out, "I'm worried about what's happening at The Chronicle."

Maryanne caught a tone in his statement that yanked her attention to Richard's face, "What's wrong?"

"Nothing yet but there is a bad storm coming at work and I'm not sure how or when it will hit us."

He quickly recounted the stories of Steam-driven printing presses in England and his bet they'd be arriving soon at his workplace. Maryanne added her own observations of the number of destitute people scooping up scraps at the market lately to confirm his fears.

Richard and Maryanne felt insulated from some of the changes that had swept the local food supply because they had a garden. It regularly supplied two thousand pounds of potatoes, fifty cabbages, and a variety of leeks, carrots and parsnips for winter use.

Richard's father had excavated a cold cellar beneath the kitchen floor when he built the house so long ago and it, coupled with the garden, allowed them to lay in supplies that most could not. The chickens and guinea fowl that kept the insects off the potatoes provided eggs and then meat when they could not all be kept through the winter. The two apple trees at the end of the garden added a coveted sweet addition to winter meals.

The family cat and dog kept mice and rats to a minimum. So, the Watson family food problems were restricted to finding oatmeal, weekly meat and fish, flour and firewood. Richard's salary easily covered those purchases – for now - but he confessed his fears of what would happen if he were let go.

"When I became a Master Printer, I convinced Mr.

Andrew to pay me a shilling on the pound for the extra work I've brought into the Print Shop through my engraving, and the book and pamphlet printing business from Grand Da' and his friends. At five percent, it doesn't dint his profits and I hate to think how rich I've made him. But it seems the way of the world. We've accumulated over twelve pounds in the wallet hanging behind the bedpost, but it won't go far if I can't get work. If I lost my job, we'd have to leave Limerick."

"For where?" Maryanne whispered.

"I have no idea!" Richard's word poured out in a torrent, "The estates are kicking the leaseholders they have, off the land so more sheep can grow where people once lived. There's no land to be had in the country. Going to Cork or Dublin or Belfast would be jumping from the frying pan into the fire. There are already hordes of people there now who can't get work. From what I hear, Limerick is one of the few places offering work on the docks in ship building or unloading the timber ships coming in from North America. I can't do manual labour because of my shoulder and …'

His words spun off into silence, "I had to share this, Maryanne because I'm really afraid. We have to start some planning and you have always been good at that."

Maryanne grasped his hand and held it tightly, "Let's think and talk more on this later," she whispered as she looked deeply into his troubled eyes.

*

"It's happening," Richard announced after dinner one night in March of 1821.

Richard and Maryanne were alone in the kitchen. The dishes had been cleared from the table. John was bedded down for the night. Richard had lit a candle and the book he was going to read lay unopened before him.

"People are walking around the shop measuring and asking which walls hold up the roof. The Steam presses are on their way – the order is already placed at the foundry and in England, some say. The new presses will be in place by summer."

Maryanne stopped her knitting, counted the completed rows on the sock she was making, then put down her work and looked at Richard carefully.

"I was talking to MacPherson," Richard continued, "at the Masonic Hall last week. He runs the ship building operation at the docks. He told me that the ships bringing his timber supplies from North America are looking for passengers for the return trip to fill up space they don't fill with china and other cargo. I'll have to find out what the fare and other accommodations, but it looks like a way to go if we must leave Limerick. His ships go to the Canada's."

"Richard, we'd never see our parents or friends, or any of our kin ever again if we do that," Maryanne said with incredulity. "It's like being exiled. What did we do wrong?"

"You're completely correct, Maryanne," replied Richard. "But the choices will be," he started ticking the alternatives off on his fingers. "We can stay here to starve slowly or quickly depending on how much work I get." Another finger was raised. "Next, I could be arrested for rioting if I protest and sent to prison or the colonies while you, John, and mother starve alone." Up went the third finger, "or lastly, we could set sail for the colonies where at least we have a choice in where we go, what we do there, and maybe when."

"You do have a talent for summary," quipped Maryanne. "How do you know there's a job for you there?"

"I don't know if you know my cousin, Ringrose Watson? He's a soldier with the Royal Artillery."

"Yes, he's the one related to the Tully's, isn't he? I know Ringrose Tully. They could hardly be other than cousins with names like that could they?" Maryanne replied.

"Well I met him in the street. He just came back from a posting to York, in Upper Canada. They were garrisoned there and spent most of their time repairing the damage from the war with the Americans a few years ago. Anyway, he had good things to say about York. It reminded him of Irishtown here without the stone buildings. Not too big, busy, lots of Irish," then added with a pause "but the same arrogant British are still in charge. I was hoping to get more out of him for the price of a pint at the pub tonight."

Maryanne shook her head in doubt, "Is this what hope costs? A pint of beer, every friend and relation we have and our life savings as well? If you can't find work, what then?" She asked starting round the track of thought again, "Will you lose your job at The Chronicle for sure?"

"I can't say. You know I've never been a part of the inner circle at the shop. I'm out on a limb that would be easy to saw off. I do know that if I am kept on, I'll be paid less."

"Have you talked to your mother about this?"

"Not yet, but I think we have to do that together."

"What is this you want to talk to me about?" asked Susannah suddenly entering the kitchen from her visit to the privy at the bottom of the garden. As Susannah closed the door and sought her chair, Maryanne broke the news.

"Richard thinks he's about to lose his job at The Chronicle because they're bringing in steam presses."

The news did not seem to surprise Susannah, "So what will you do then?" she asked.

"We may have to leave Limerick," Richard said.

Susannah eased into her chair. A few squeaks from

the rocker filled the pause before Susannah replied, "I won't be doing that, Richard. But you and your family would betray everything I've worked for if you stay here to…I can see what's happening already with the weavers. We grandparents talk of nothing else. Because of your education and skills, you have chances that few others have on the street. You must use them to save yourself and continue the family. Nothing is more important than that. That is your duty." She stopped for a breath.

"At my age, I'll not be moving anywhere. I'll die in this house. So, let me free you from any obligations you may feel towards me. Parents raise children to leave them. If you must leave, you will only be realizing the dream and effort of your mother who tried to get you ready for this moment." Susannah looked calmly from Richard to Maryanne.

"But we'd never see you again," whispered Maryanne.

"That's so, my dear," she said reaching across the space and clasping Maryanne's hands between her own and looking straight into her eyes. "But it would happen someday anyway. If you must go, it will be a gift to me to see you off safely while I'm able and sane."

"How will you live alone here?" Maryanne asked as Susannah rocked back, her handclasp broken.

"If you leave, I'll talk to Sarah and her husband. Maybe they could move in. We all know they've outgrown the place they have down the street. If they came here, they could attend the store from here. I doubt they'll be moving anywhere because he owns his own shop."

Nobody ever received such a blessing with such a heavy heart.

*

"I have a reply to my letter last Fall to the Upper Canada Gazette." Richard announced and laid the unopened letter on the table.

Maryanne sat at the other end of the table. John squirmed on the bench between them. Susannah beside him, sat as still as stone.

"I'm afraid to open it," Richard said.

"Fate turns on small things," said Susannah

"Will you open it and read it?" Richard asked Susannah

Without a word, she picked it up and broke the seal.

*

"So, there you are! Mr. ...," Susannah glanced back at the letter on the table, "Fothergill offers you a job as a printer working with equipment like you've been using here, depending on how well you work. Looking back at the letter she continued, "He even lists the details of ships to take, and the Boarding House you might use

when you get there – on Queen street no less! Mr.
Watson's recommendation from The Chronicle must
have carried some weight."

Richard simply sat with his head down in silence.

"The family has never been short on courage,
Richard Watson. I know I can count on yours now,"
Susannah said as she stretched out a hand to grasp
Richard's, "And you too dear," she said as she reached to
clasp Maryanne's.

Richard reached his other hand the length of the table to
grasp Maryanne's and so linked in a circle, they looked
from one to another in silence. It was Susannah who
broke the moment by saying, "And you too young man."

She took her hand from Maryanne and gave it to John
beside her, who had been the silent and surprised witness
to what had happened.

"Give your other hand to your mother," Susannah
directed, and John did. "Go in peace and certainty with
the courage and conviction you carry from your heritage.
Testing times are before us all. But we will all meet
them as those at Dunkeld did. Remember whose name
you carry.

9
LEAVING LIMERICK

The six weeks after receiving the letter inviting him to
York to work in the shop of the Upper Canada Gazette
were a scramble for Richard and Maryanne. They had to
prepare for events they could only imagine. They had
decided against separate passage that might separate
them for years. They would go as a family.

Their savings of seventeen pounds, twelve shillings, six
pence was eaten into by a series of purchases the first of
which were three seaman's trunks. Maryanne began the
task of filling them with what she imagined they would
need - fabric for future clothes, dishes layered between
the cloth, kitchen utensils and maybe a treasure or two
that would come with them. Everyone got another pair of
boots made by Maryanne's father and their old shoes
were re-soled. Richard bought engraving tools, some
sheet copper, a pound of the best beeswax, a small bottle
of acid, a few quills and ink along with a few sheets of
parchment, that could be cut up for any purpose. It was
so little to support so much.

"Seal the acid and ink bottles in separate pig's bladders as well pack them in boxes so they don't crush," cautioned Richard.

In Maryanne 's trunk were new kitchen knives; a steel and strop joined the trunk collection. John Bennis, the blacksmith, replaced the worn blade in Richard's well-honed penknife for another decade of use at least. Susannah also insisted that Maryanne take twenty pounds of seed potatoes to plant in their new home. The winter-weight socks Susannah knit for the family were filled with oats for milling then stuffed into a new large iron pot like Susannah's for the trip. Two new ladles lay in the trunk below the pot. Bennis gave Maryanne a small hand mill by which she could grind the oats, or, if she changed the perforated plate and blade, meat for sausage etc. It looked like a useful tool, and proved so in the kitchen, so it was packed up.

Deep down one side of the trunk, Maryanne secreted her sewing kit with scissors, needles – lots of needles - and buttons - lots and lots of buttons – white and dark, large and small. Ribbons and lace trim, all the notions that she expected would be hard to find were forced to fit beside the kit. And thread. She stocked up on English cotton thread and even more thread of Irish linen. Wool for sweaters and socks padded everything not covered by fabric. Three sizes of knitting needles filled space between the ladles.

At the bottom of Richard's trunk were a new shovel blade, a mattock blade and a hoe head.

"Get the handles in North America," Bennis had said, "I hear thy have lots of wood."

One of the last items that made it into the trunk was a tightly lidded small pot of Irish soil from the garden. On top of the pot was placed a small envelope of shamrock seeds. Susannah had the potter make the pot square so that it fit into the corner of the trunk. Envelopes of carrot and other garden vegetable seeds were added to the shamrocks and finally a vial of apples seeds was wrapped into an oilcloth pouch. Susannah also insisted they take the short shoots she had rooted from the Apple trees and had set into a clay cylinder filled with damp moss.

"Just water it with drinking water, never saltwater," she cautioned.

Richard had paid the seven pounds their passage would cost, to the ship's owners, and at his insistence, been shown the accommodation. He had expected their room to be Spartan. He was not prepared for the shelf he was shown below decks. Surrounding a space smaller than his kitchen, was a wide shelf running around the gloomy hold of the ship. The shelf created spaces above and below it, each about three feet high. The spaces were divided by vertical partitions about five feet apart. Each box-shaped space was for a different family he was told. There were ten spaces on each side of the hold.

"Crew and cargo are aft," explained the mate as Richard looked about the space again, struggling with the commitment he had made for himself and his family.

The space for the family was perhaps five feet wide and deep and hardly three feet high. When Richard said he'd take the upper bunk, the mate wrote 'WATSON' on a paper and tacked it to the corner post of the space as he said, "Good choice! Sea sickness, you know."

That thought had not crossed his mind. What was sea sickness? The mate didn't mention that the upper bunk was first to get the water that might come through a leaky deck seam.

"Where does our luggage go?" Richard had asked.

"In there with you," was the mate's reply.

Richard couldn't help but gasp. "That is less space than in the cart that will bring us," he shouted.

"Well an aft cabin above decks costs fourteen pounds and there is one left," offered the mate.

That ended the conversation. The fare Richard had paid would get them to Quebec City but beyond, he had been told by Mr. Fothergill in Toronto, there was another two or three weeks of travel by steamer and stagecoach and then sailing ship on Lake Ontario. The cost for those legs would be close to another three, maybe four pounds for the family and that did not include the cost of feeding everyone after they reached Quebec. The total costs would leave them almost nothing to establish themselves in York. They would arrive virtually destitute and without the fare to come back.

Richard re-measured the size of their space in the hold of the ship comparing it with the size of the trunks they had already bought. He mentally stacked two trunks high and wedged them with one sideways. John could sleep in the slot left above that last trunk. He and Maryanne would sleep spoon-style.

"Cooking is on deck when the captain allows," instructed the mate. "He'll show you where you can set up common cooking fires for you all. If we have bad weather, we eat cold rations. You can see your provisions are part of your fare," directing Richard's attention to the small print in the corner of his ticket that was all but invisible in the gloom.

"Toilet facilities?" asked Richard.

"Well in good weather you use the lee rail," the mate said. "There'll be a canvas set up for the ladies and modesty and all. In bad weather…" He pulled aside a dingy tattered curtain surrounding a space under the ladder to the deck to reveal a pail.

"Is that for sixty people?" croaked Richard hoarsely.

"Maybe eighty," replied the mate

Richard returned home absolutely discouraged. How could he ever have gotten his family into such a mess?

How would he ever explain this to Maryanne? He was leaning his head against the doorpost of his house hesitating to go in, when Maryanne, with a large wicker marketing basket over her arm, came up behind him. She touched his shoulder and reached past him to open the door.

"You look like you're holding up the world."

"Maryanne, I've doomed us."

"Sounds bad," Maryanne said casually and pushing past him into the kitchen to put down her market basket on the preparation counter.

She turned to hang her shawl of black wool knit in a fisherman's pattern on the peg behind the door. Richard sagged into his chair at the table as the ticket fell from his hand.

"It's awful," he said. "To get to North America, we have to live and sleep in a space about this big," he said holding out his arms wide.

"Richard, I know that. You should go to the market more. You find out all sorts of things there."

Then sitting down on the bench at the side of the table and reaching for his hand she said softly, "Richard, it is a test. Did you not hear your Mother the other day? It is a test of our courage. How often have we been over this? If we are to survive, we must do this, and we will. And what a story it will give us. Do you know an Irishman who doesn't like a story? Well this will be ours.

It is why I bought this basket today," Maryanne said.

She proudly flipped back the wicker lid.

"Everything we will need for everyday will go in here. The trunks will stay closed for the trip. We'll wear winter coats and cloaks one over the other and won't need blankets. I'm going to sew two aprons together and wear them. I can fill the space between with wool to knit along the way. I'll look like an ox, but never mind. I have a small pot for meals, and spoons to eat whatever we prepare in it. Here's a small kitchen knife. You've got your penknife. Each of us gets one change of shirt and socks. Your mother's apple tree cuttings go in this slot, laundry soap here."

She showed him a large paper-wrapped square, "Here's where I'll pack my wool and needles for knitting day to day."

Richard was bedazzled by the organization, but his spirits began to lift because of it. Maryanne picked up the ticket and noted in the corner, the food that would be provided:

"Three and a half pounds of biscuit for each of us," she read, "Three and a half pounds of oatmeal or 15 lb. potato per week and 3 quarts of water a day for each of us and half rations for John. We'll get by on that. I don't see any meat."

"They probably sell it on board."

"I wonder about taking a small keg of salt pork

with us," she mused, "Well I'll fit our coats with inside pockets and carry all the carrots we can."

There will be a light in that ship, and it would be his wife, Richard decided.

10
STARTING IN YORK

Richard clumped up the outside staircase to the door of their apartment after a full day at the Upper Canada Gazette. It was mid July 1822. He scraped the street mud from his boots on the edge of the top step then took them off and set them beside the door as he entered. Maryanne was staring out the window towards the lake in the distance. He could smell dinner cooking on the iron woodstove.

Two days after their arrival in Toronto, they'd found two rooms to rent over a dry goods store on south side of King Street. It was within walking distance of the King's Printer that printed all Government documents and a weekly newspaper. It was where Charles Fothergill employed Richard.

Behind the two-storey clapboard in which they had the upstairs apartment, was a pleasant south-facing space. Richard and Maryanne had been allowed to plant a garden there. Though it was late for planting when they arrived and the potatoes were well sprouted, they planted them as soon as they could. About twenty pounds of left-over local seed potatoes, well past their best, supplemented the planting. Maryanne had nursed their carrot seeds into seedlings but she was constantly tending the plants to keep insects off so the plants could thrive. It was too late to plant cabbages when they arrived. The chickens they had in Limerick were not affordable.

There was no fencing for the garden and the wild animals would have made quick work of any birds not securely enclosed. When Maryanne asked why some of the potato sprouts had been eaten off, their neighbour, Harold Price, told her about rabbits. He showed her how to set snares and by week's end, two rabbits were in the pot.

Maryanne immediately began to plan a fence made of panels of tightly woven willow branches. The apple tree cuttings had survived the trip and were now enclosed by short lengths of stovepipe to protect them from mice. Maryanne had planted them close by the building on each corner of the house giving them protection against north winds and the blessing of reflected warmth from the wall. Their landlord advised them that some sort of arbour would need to be built around them till they grew tall enough to escape the appetite of winter deer who blundered into town.

"Would a dog help with that?" Richard asked Harold, thinking of their terrier at home.

"Good idea, but let's see if they get past the mice."

It was all idyll talk to fill the silence that surrounded their days now. Richard and Maryanne laboured in the garden every night and sometimes, when they finished, exhausted, Maryanne would lean into him and just cry and cry. In those moments, Richard wondered if his own heart would break. He could only hold her shaking shoulders against his own and wait for the emotional storm to pass.

In each of their heads rushed the memory of the bright sun, the light rolling of the ship, the patter of wind-driven spray splashing across the deck from the bow. Behind that moment came the next memory of the squeals of laughter as the children ran back and forth trying to dodge the droplets.

Then the squeak of a slipped foot on the deck, the cry as the child fell through the open hatch, the terrible crack of a head hitting the ladder and then the thud as the body hit the deck amidst the parents talking quietly from their bunks in the hold around the hatch. There was a thunderous silence and then a scramble to catch up the unmoving child, an unearthly scream from Maryanne when she found it was John.

"Broke his neck when he fell," the doctor said. "Killed in an instant."

And then the burial at sea - was there a worst nightmare than that? The white canvas shroud made by the sailor who sewed John into it, the ballast rock at the foot. Both remembered the feel of the crowd bumping them as the captain read the service while the ship rolled, and the spray flicked their faces. The words stopped and, in the silence, came that horrible splash then Maryanne's scream that unleashed the weeping that went on and on.

Exhausted, Maryanne stopped weeping aloud, but the pain in her eyes showed she continued to weep inside. Even now, the first sprinkles of a summer shower on her face would bring a cry to her throat. The only way to banish the ringing silence of the childless home they now shared seemed to be manic attention to the garden.

Maryanne hoed and hilled and watered the potatoes with a zeal her neighbours understood. A horse did not pass on the road, but its droppings were collected and worked into the sandy soil in more digging and spreading. When they had unpacked, Maryanne could not open John's trunk. It was her neighbour, Helen Price, who said that those clothes needed to be aired after the trip and if Maryanne would let her, she would help by doing that.

"They will mold and spoil and that shouldn't happen. Let me help you in this," Helen offered.

With tears streaming down her face, and trying to choke a sob, Maryanne nodded. Helen had taken the trunk home in her wheelbarrow then washed and dried everything on a clothesline set up on the other side of her house so Maryanne could not see. When Helen returned the clean and dry clothes, she brought a pitcher of water and glasses and sat with Maryanne as the grieving mother talked about each piece she folded and replaced reverently in the trunk.

"You'll have another someday," Helen had said knowingly. "Have hope, Maryanne. Would you like me to write your kin in Limerick? They will want to know you arrived."

"I would be grateful if you would. I can't do that now. Please say to Mr. Bennis, that the grinder works well and to my mother that the seeds and potatoes survived. Please tell her the apple trees leafed out."

The Price's offered them storage space in their own root cellar for five large bags of potatoes and 2 bags of carrots. The rest of the produce, they sold for oatmeal for the winter. The first winter, Richard and Maryanne put out the candle right after supper. In one of their dark-time conversations at bedtime, Richard tried to plan how he could join those who ran the town's business rather than be their victim.

One of the first steps, he decided would be to join St. James Anglican Church. From his work at The Gazette, he had learned that this was the church attended by influential people. And so, they made the long walk on Sunday mornings, to see and be seen.

*

It helped that the Price's attended the same church as well, so they found it pleasurable to walk together with them to Sunday Morning Service. On this fine Fall day, breezes that lifted a little dust from the street were cool on the face. Sun that dazzled from a blue sky was warm on the back.

Maryanne and Helen were walking home side-by-side with their husbands walking behind when Helen confessed, "I'm going to have another baby."
Maryanne stopped.

She glanced up at Helen and the flash of concern was buried in a beaming smile of congratulation so big, it might have lit up the street.

"That's wonderful," squealed Maryanne.

"I was worried how you'd feel," said Helen a bit anxiously.

"Well it brings me joy to know that my blackness has not touched you," Maryanne said. "And because you have been so caring for me, I think I am almost recovered from the depths to which John's death took me. I look forward to sharing your excitement and helping all I can."

A silent breath was not taken for the rest of their walk home. The men didn't seem to notice, so deep were they in their own discussion. Richard had taken another step towards integration into the social life of York. It happened when he thought he received a secret Masonic handshake after Church two weeks earlier. Richard followed the introduction and handshake with an open-ended question about Men's groups and that led Walter Rose, to whom he had been introduced, to ask if he had heard of Freemasonry.

The invitation was extended to meet during the next week at the local Hall. Richard was feeling apprehensive and apologetic when he opened the door at the Masonic Hall that night. He'd brought with him his regalia such as it was, from Limerick only to find he was enthusiastically welcomed like a lost brother. He was surprised and encouraged at the appreciation he felt, by those who made big decisions in the city.

Richard struggled to recall the names of the men to whom he was introduced that night. Most were British. He did not hear another Irish lilt in the room. So, he thought it prudent to ask questions and let others tell him about the city in which he found himself.

The topic of Freemasonry came up between himself and Harold Price as they walked home behind their wives who were talking so animatedly ahead of them that Sunday morning. Richard had so little to talk about, he found. To him, the Sermons he'd heard relied more on volume and vocabulary for impact, than Christian kindness. But it was not an opinion he felt he could share. It was the ideas of brotherhood and universality that had drawn him originally to the Masons. He didn't know if he could share that with Harold.

But he opened with the usual question, "Do you know anything about Freemasonry?"

British-born Harold Price was a contractor. He was working flat out building houses in York for wealthy immigrants who seemed to arrive in numbers by the day. He was interested to hear that Richard's father had been a

Master Builder in Limerick. They shared some common problems, talking about drawings and architects, egos and imagination as they walked along. But it was obvious to Richard that Harold had just been mulling over the Mason question as they had filled the time talking about the other topics.

"I'd be interested to talk further about it," Harold offered eventually.

Richard had replied almost identically to the invitation his father had issued back in Limerick and it ended the same way. He accompanied Harold on Thursday night to the Mason's meeting at the Hall. Richard had already sensed Harold's interest was rooted in possible commercial connections.

*

Helen bore a son in the spring, and they named him Henry Price.

"He's going to be a lawyer," said Harold Price over drinks at the Hall. Fellow Masons lifted glasses on all sides to cheer the new father.

"Hear! Hear!" said all.

*

Richard thought he recognized from St. James Church, the face that greeted him from the front door at the offices of The Gazette.

"I was told I could have some invitations printed here," said the imposing woman standing there.

Black lace over a dark blue skirt and jacket had caught Richard's attention. The ruffles of a white blouse led upwards to a broad face set with brown eyes. White ruffles at her cuffs balanced the dark blue straw hat under which most of her brown hair was hidden.

"It would be my pleasure' ma'am," said Richard rising from the stool and tall desk where he had been proof-reading copy for next week's edition.

Richard picked up a collection of sample invitations and guided the customer to a nearby table where he spread them for the lady's evaluation. A quarter hour was spent choosing this script, and that wording, and the other arrangements of the text. When he thought she had finalized her decisions, Richard took a fresh piece of card stock from a convenient stack on the table, lifted a quill pen from its holder beside the paper and dipped the tip into the bottle of ink at hand.

"What name goes in the first line?" Richard inquired.

"Sir John Harvey and Lady Harvey," she said with a lift of her chin.

Without the least pause Richard smoothly included the name into the composition upon which she had decided.

"Yes, that looks quite acceptable," she sighed. Richard immediately sensed the hesitation. He dipped his pen again.

"Could I suggest a decorative addition to the side?" And drew a smooth flourishing curve along the left margin.

"Oh yes, that makes such a statement, don't you think? That looks wonderful," she enthused. "I didn't see that on the other samples."

"I didn't do those samples," said Richard. "I've only recently begun here."

"Will all the invitations look like this?" she asked.

"Yes, Lady Harvey. We'll engrave a plate so that they all will look exactly like this," assured Richard.

"Well with work like this, I'm sure you will do well," she held out the card admiringly at arm's length. "But you must assure me that you will not use this decoration on anyone else's work."

"Of course, Lady Harvey," Richard nodded with a smile. As he was writing down the number of invitations on the order form, Richard asked, "Might we prepare a unique letterhead for new stationery recognizing your husband's recent knighthood?"

As she left the office having ordered new writing paper as well, Richard wondered how difficult it might be to suggest to Maryanne that they name a son, *John Harvey Watson*. He rehearsed how he hoped the conversation might go; "The 'John' will recognize my Great Grandfather, and our first child – neither name nor the memory will die that way. And we could add a middle name as some of the wealthy do. It's becoming fashionable you know. We'd chose someone we admire and respect."

"And who is Mr. Harvey?"

He'd have to answer with confidence, "He's the Lieutenant Colonel who commanded at the Battle of Stoney Creek back in 1813. Without him, this would be American soil now and we'd likely be starving in Limerick."

"Hmmmm," she'd say, "but don't you think there's something we must do before we start naming children?"

11
MOVING UP IN TORONTO

Helen Price had a son that gave Maryanne hope. The boy
had been born safely before Maryanne confessed to her
friend that she too was pregnant and had been for 3
months but was afraid to say anything to Helen just
because….

"When your first child dies, you can never forget,"
Helen had sympathized. "But you will find joy with this
one I'm sure, just as you did with John," Helen replied
when the news was shared.

Maryanne bore a daughter in the late summer of 1824.
They named the child Sarah after Richard's mother's
nickname and his sister in Limerick. It was a delicate
time for Maryanne. Even though the pregnancy went
normally - well as normal as anything unique usually
goes – Maryanne had trouble assuring herself that this
time, the child was not being granted on loan.

"Will God come to reclaim her as he did with
John?" asked Maryanne in tears one night.

"How can you believe in a whimsical God like that?" had been Richard's tender reply.

Maryanne was pleased to share child-minding with Helen in the weeks that followed baby Sarah's birth and time flew by.

*

"Whoa," said Richard Watson and tugged on the reins of the horse pulling the wagon back from the docks in Toronto. "Isn't that Jim Lumsden?" He works at the Colonial Advocate. God, he looks in terrible shape."

"Here," he said to Ian McTavish beside him on the wagon, "you take the wagon back to the shop and be sure all those bundles of paper go right inside. It feels like rain and we can't lose this load. We'll be struggling to meet our needs even with this consignment from Crooks in Dundas. You know the ship from England sank with this year's supply, don't you?"

Ian didn't know that but it hardly mattered. He followed directions well and left the reasons to others. Richard handed the reins to Ian and hopped down from the box into the muddy street. He turned back the way he had come to see if it was Jim moving slowly towards him but before he let go his grip on the wagon, he reminded Ian, to be sure the horse were taken back to the livery as well.

"Yes sir," replied Ian as he flicked the reins and the wagon pulled away.

"Jim, is it you under there?" Richard called as he approached the bandaged figure limping towards him.

A brown eye peeked from beneath the hood of bandages that was visible beneath his hat. Black bruising continued down the man's cheek beyond the bandage that covered his left eye and ear. There was only one button holding the torn coat closed.

"It is," was the hoarse answer.

"Here sit down." Richard drew him to the bench in front of the hardware store. "You look pretty much the worse for wear."

"It's amazing what boots and an axe handle will do," Jim groaned as he slid slowly down store's window frame onto the seat. "Those buggers really put it to me. Maybe we should just have beat it out the back door when they came in the front, but we couldn't leave Mrs. Mackenzie and her son to face the thugs alone."

Jim coughed up some stuff and groaned as he held his side. Richard twisted towards Jim and pulled his feet from the path of passers-by on the boardwalk.

"I heard it was a bunch of Indians that broke in while the boss was away."

"Is that what they say at your place? Well that's a lie! It was a bunch of scoundrels from the Law Society – the young kids who are working for the lawyers downtown. They had dressed up to look like Indians but I, and everyone else, knows every one of them. I think if you visit Sam Jarvis's office, you'll see the apprentice that had the long nose down which he'd look at us, now has a nose as wide a two-lane street. And over at the Attorney General's office, is another Clerk with a black eye courtesy of this," Jim held up his bruised right fist. "But there were too many of them for the few of us. They wrecked the press, Richard – broke the frame with sledges and threw the type in the harbour while the Lord High Attorney General, John Bloody Robinson himself stood outside and waved them on," Jim wheezed passionately. "I did keep them from setting fire to the place, though. Grabbed the torch from the hands of one lout and stuffed it back into his face before I threw it out into a puddle outside. That singed his whiskers," Jim said around a cough. "That's when I saw the Attorney General and the Solicitor General themselves and William Allan president of the Upper Canada Bank as well. It was like they'd been selling tickets at their club."

Jim was breathless by the time he finished ranting and groaned as he gripped his broken ribs.

"So, it wasn't a bunch of drunks and rowdies?"

It was a surprise to Richard.

"Don't you believe it! These are the dogs let loose by our government that are trying to silence Mr. Mackenzie for all the pointed editorials he's had us set lately. Did anyone write up an article at Gazette?" Jim inquired through clenched teeth.

"Not a peep," replied Richard.

"Well don't be surprised if you hear more about this attack," promised Jim. "Though a dozen people could name the eight thugs, not one will be charged. But it won't end there. I hear Mackenzie is going to bring a civil suit against the brigands. Mackenzie is not going to let them get away with this and if he has his way, the Family Compact, as he calls them, will pay for him to fight them for the next 20 years with the damages he'll claim."

"Are you up to a bit of food?" asked Richard, as Jim recovered his breath. "Join me at Graham's Tavern for some lunch. It's just up the street a block or so."

Jim raised his single eye and studied Richard carefully. After a couple breaths, he agreed, "I'd be grateful for that sir."

Together they made their way up the street for soup and a small loaf. Richard left with the bill after being sure Jim had a small ale to smooth out his aches then trudged back to the office of the Upper Canada Gazette. Richard dodged through the door just as the first sprinkles fell. He was pleased to see the box of the wagon was empty and the bundles of fresh paper for the printing of the next few weeks stacked carefully inside and the horses not stamping impatiently.

Charles Fothergill was pronouncing with the authority of the ignorant on the quality of what Crooks had sent him.

"Definitely inferior quality," huffed Forthergill.

"Look how rough it is!"

"We can cope," Richard assured him. "We'll just be more careful with the ink. It will set up just fine. You'll see. And it will be a site better than what anyone will recover of our shipment from England from the wreck."

Fothergill was not amused. He set off on another rant about not having enough paper for the coming reports he was required, as King's Printer, to produce for the government.

Well in for a penny, in for a pound, thought Richard. Though this was the man who had offered him a job to come to, and all the security of continued employment, the man was rabidly self-centered. Richard tried to keep the man from irrational decisions, but sometimes, he just liked to tweet the lion's tail. Richard continued the conversation by suggesting that he thought there might be a supply of paper he could obtain from Eastwood's Paper Mill out on the Don River.

And sure enough, the ensuing explosion about quality and having to deal with pirates who would extort every penny from him knowing his misfortune, was worth the suggestion.

"Have you thought of petitioning the Council for an increase in their payments to cover these higher local costs? Maybe a surcharge on the English paper would encourage our local suppliers to invest in improved equipment so we don't have to bring the paper we need from halfway around the world?" Asked Richard.

"Odd you should mention that, Watson," replied Fothergill. "I'm told that my submission to the Executive Council has just been approved. They'll be paying me by the page now, instead of at a flat rate. So, this year's annual report will be printed with the 16-point type and you'll triple space the lines."

"Pardon?" queried Richard, sure that he had not heard correctly. "Sir, that type size is what we use for headlines in the smaller articles in the newspaper. We usually use 10-point type."

"I'll use the inferior quality of the paper to justify the wider spacing and larger letters. Most of the old fogies can't see as well as they used to anyway. That's another reason for increasing the type size and spacing," he declared with false concern," *and higher profit for me,* he thought.

"If we use 16-point type for the text, sir, we'll have to use 24-point for the chapter headings. I'm not sure we'll have enough. If we have to recover the type before we can print the next page, it may take longer to produce the Report," Richard cautioned.

"Yes," chuckled Fothergill. "That will be fine."

In his mind, Richard did the arithmetic on the job.

"This will cost close to nine hundred pounds to do!

That's more than ten times last year's cost!" Richard warned.

"It's already been approved," smiled Fothergill

"Bandits and Rogues all," mused Richard as he looked out through the rain-streaked window. "Will we be including an article in this week's paper about the destruction of Mr. Mackenzie's press at the Colonial Advocate?" Richard asked.

"Why?" asked Fothergill. "It was drunken hoodlums," I understand. "We don't want to advertise such behaviour, do we? There are already enough who would take such a report as encouragement. I'd like you to prepare an item about the punishment of the horse thieves and the public lashing that will occur on Wednesday next."

"Yes sir," sighed Richard as he walked away.

*

Richard was now regularly involved in the administration of the St. George's Masonic Lodge to which he belonged. With Walter Rose, he arranged for the renting of the hall to Baptists. That was only the first of many matters to which Richard was invited to contribute. Richard was not then surprised to be asked by Grand Master Carfrae one evening after the regular meeting, to meet with him and William Lyon Mackenzie, his colleague in the printing business, and Jim Lumsden's boss, in a side room off the main hall.

It was slightly warmer in the room than the cool Fall evening outside. The fireplace had not been lit, so the meeting would be brief. Oil lamps lit the room enough to convey comfort.

"You know each other?" Carfrae asked.

"Yes, Sir," said Richard. "The Colonial Advocate has a reputation for pointed print around town. Good Evening, Mr. Mackenzie."

"I'm pleased to hear that, especially from one working at the Upper Canada Gazette," acknowledged Mackenzie. "But what's this I hear about Mr. Fothergill pillaging the public purse – again?"

"I'd rather not discuss my employer's practices Sir, but amongst we three, I'd be pleased if you would," Richard replied cautiously.

Nodding at Mackenzie, Carfrae said "You wrote something recently that interested me." Carfrae held up a folded broadsheet to the light and squinting, read, "It was preposterous to perpetuate sectarianism even beyond the grave," and further on…. Carfrae crinkled the paper, squinted and read again, "There should be a public burial place for all classes and sects. Do you believe that?"

"I only write what I believe," Mackenzie huffed indignantly.

To diffuse the fuse, he had accidentally lit under

Mackenzie, Carfrae quickly turned to Richard, "What about you Mr. Watson?"

While Richard replied, Carfrae lit up a cigar. Surprised by the question, Richard paused to put his thoughts in order.

"We buried a child at sea gentlemen. There can be no more universal place than that. I have thought long since, that squabbles over one's religion at a time of death are a tragic reminder of our human frailty or pigheadedness."

The silence with which Richard's words were considered had the calming effect Carfrae had hoped for.

After a reverent pause Carfrae went on, "We agree then?" he said, looking into the eyes of each in turn. Nods came from both. "I thought that the Lodge might lead a public subscription towards obtaining land for a cemetery that would act under those principals. A piece of property that might be suitable up Yonge Street has come to my attention. But before proceeding, I wanted to get a sense of how the members might respond to a request for donations. And Watson, the fastest way to learn that seems to start with you. You seem to have a good knowledge of the membership, and they seem to comment favourably about you. What do you think?"

"How much would the land cost?" Richard asked. "The cost will determine the number of donors we might need and the scale of each contribution."

"I'd guess about seventy or eighty pounds would do. We won't have to raise all that. I want to petition the legislature to acquire the property but if it was known that we had already raised some funds, it might convey the public's support and alert the slower of thought in Government of the coming decision."

"Can I quote you on that?" chuckled Mackenzie.

"Only as an unnamed source," smiled Carfrae.

Richard interjected, "I'd start by asking some of our wealthier members for maybe ten shillings towards the project," mused Richard. "If we could get several of them to start the donations and tell them that the highest donors name will be at the top of the list, even if they donate anonymously, that might encourage others to contribute."

"You do have a talent for motivation," joked Carfrae. "I know to whose vanity you'll be appealing. You might even offer the higher placement in a silent contest between them. I'm pretty sure that might work. When could you start?"

"Well, I could print up a poster for next week but maybe I could start collecting pledges tonight if I tour the bar."

"No grass growing under your feet eh!" said Carfrae with wave of his cigar.

"Right. Will I put you down for 15 shillings or

more?" Richard asked Mackenzie as he wiggled a notepad and pencil from his pocket. Stunned, the craggy face glared back at him. "Well you can't honestly print those words and not stand behind them, can you?" Richard asked.

It took a moment for Mackenzie to recover, "I think ten shillings will start the bidding well enough, Sir," Mackenzie replied frostily.

"Mr. Carfrae?" asked Richard.
There was a small pause as Carfrae blew smoke towards the ceiling.

"Twelve," Carfrae said quietly and drew on his cigar again as he watched Mackenzie squirm, just a bit.

"Well then," Carfrae concluded. "That's settled!"

Mackenzie rose with a nod to both and marched to the door. Carfrae's touch held Richard in his seat till Mackenzie was through the door.

"Let me know how things are going in a few weeks, Watson. And by the way, would you and your wife be our guests for Hogmanay?"

"It would be our pleasure, I'm sure." Richard replied with a handshake.

*

Was it the passionate lovemaking after the New Year's

Eve celebration that led Maryanne to find herself pregnant again? She was never sure, but she recalled the night fondly. Coach rides and compliments; candlelight, and crystal; that was how she summarized the evening to Helen Price. And again, Maryanne thanked Helen for her help in finding a dressmaker to make a gown like Maryanne had never had in her life.

"If that is how Cinderella felt when she went to the ball, it is no wonder the tale made it into a book," she sighed recalling one of her reading lessons in faraway Limerick.

Maryanne bore a son on Sept 13, 1827 and having toyed with the name for a couple years, she and Richard named the baby John Harvey Watson as Richard had proposed. Richard was not ashamed to announce the child's name at the Masonic Hall or buy the requisite round of drinks after the regular meeting. He noticed the approving nods from Grandmaster Carfrae and the others from the militia who noted immediately, the memorializing of their hero of the Battle of Stoney Creek.

*

Richard was talking to Robert Stanton, newly appointed King's Printer after Fothergill's extravagant printing costs and change of political direction had driven him into disgrace and distant employment.

"Yes sir! We can easily print this year's report on local paper, with regular 10-point type at about one tenth the cost of last year."

Stanton, who had lobbied for and won the job, had no idea how to print a newspaper. Whatever his shortcomings, Richard appreciated Stanton's energy and even more that he had recognized Richard's skill and broad knowledge. He had promoted Richard to confidential foreman. That promotion came with a dramatic increase in pay.

With more money, Richard could look for new accommodation for his growing family. Maryanne was pregnant again. Coincidentally, Harold Price, their long-time friend and property developer had just finished a new block of row housing – brick buildings set back from the street to allow for a modest porch to sit on and enjoy evenings when the weather was hot and humid.

There was a back yard that faced south and for Maryanne that had been the clinching attraction. Richard put his name on the mortgage. She did love her garden. Having the Prices as almost neighbours at the end of the block was the finishing touch as far as she was concerned.

For Richard, the four bedrooms, a parlour with a fireplace, another fireplace in the master bedroom and space for a large wood-fired range in the kitchen that could heat the bedrooms above through an ornamental metal grill in the ceiling had been the important selling points. Richard did not suffer winter's chill well.

*

"Will we be reporting Mr. Mackenzie's settlement

for the damage done to the Colonial Advocate last year?"
Richard asked to break out of his own daydream. It was
a surprise to hear how that worked out. "It would boost
our readership. There's a lot of interest in the streets," he
offered Mr. Stanton.

"Remind me how that ended," he asked.

"Well he turned down an offer of £200 to settle
and opted for a jury trial. The jury awarded him £625!
Can you imagine that? With the new press he's bought
and paid for, he could be set for life," Richard speculated.
He continued, "And if we publish that, we'd better
publish Strachan's latest diatribe. He's laying into the
Methodists and Mr. Ryerson with vigour. It will help to
present the paper in a manner that appeals to everyone
and draws sales from both sides on the street. If we put
Strachan's headline in larger type, it will keep the
subscribers happy, I think," Richard continued. "As well,
increased circulation will attract more advertisers and
that is good for the balance sheet." *Any conversation that
ended in more money seemed to make these people
happy*, thought Richard.

"I think Mr. Strachan is embarrassed to find
someone doing a count and declaring there are more
Methodists in Toronto than Anglicans," observed
Stanton. "I doubt much time will pass before we see a
rebuttal from Ryerson. Strachan's charges verge on libel,
in my mind."

"You are undoubtedly correct, Sir," commented
Richard.

"I like your suggestions and the balance you offer, Watson, as long as our thumb keeps the balance where it is. You understand my meaning," Stanton said with a sidelong look and raised eyebrow?

"Completely sir."

"See to it then," said Stanton as he picked up his top hat and cane and headed for the door.

12
BECOMING PART OF THE ESTABLISHMENT

The news fell like an anvil in the shop, "The Cholera is back."

Even Stanton's ears went up as he caught the ominous word through the open door of his office. He rose from his desk and stepped quickly into the other room. The other printers and apprentices stopped and turned as the boss came towards Richard who had just made the announcement. Richard set down the ink and steel pen nibs he'd just brought from the Stationary Supplies beside the orders for new work on the counter.

"How do you know?" demanded Mr. Stanton.

"The hospital is asking us to print more admission forms, a lot more," replied Richard pointing to a sheaf of order forms on the counter.

"I heard from the Stationers that they want more ink and pen nibs as well," Richard declared. "And as I came back, I met the Quartermaster from the Fort. They've been asked to assemble tents and deliver them to the hospital by next week. He also said that Captain Carfrae had ordered shovels and lime to be sent in barrel lots to the new cemetery. Soldiers will be digging trench graves," Richard added.

Everyone was stunned by the facts and were trying to put them together in any other way.

"The Stationary Store manager says he's lost two employees from Cabbage Town and every bed in the hospital is full at this very moment," Richard concluded.

"I thought we might have escaped this year, but it appears not the case," sighed Stanton.

"It's those bloody immigrants you know. They brought the plague with them!" Muttered Ian as he left the room headed for the Press.

He knew what was coming. Paper and ink had to be pulled from storage. The press had to be checked that it was clean and working.

To Richard, Stanton directed, "Send someone over to the Legislature to ask if there are plans to hire wagons and men to collect bodies. If this goes the way it's gone before, we'll have to start gathering the dead from the hospital and maybe in the community by next week. Let's see who's in charge so we can print up what the public is expected to know."

"Right away sir! Ian, look lively there," Richard called out as their general labourer came back in from the next room.

*

Richard brought the news home to Maryanne that night. He hadn't taken off his boots at the door, nor hung up his hat before he told her.

"The rumours have been flying for days now," she said, "but I hadn't heard how quickly things had spread. Your news from the militia and the hospital confirms it."

Maryanne stirred the pot on the stove and stepped to the cupboard for soda bread to go with the evening's stew. A pitcher followed to the table and the whiff left in its passing said it did not contain water.

"Well it is small beer for everyone – no water for a while, and strong tea." Maryanne was issuing the orders for the family and her tone said there would be no argument.

She had long ago decided that there was something about the disease connected to water, hence her directive to Richard. Richard knew enough not to debate the topic. Fact or fantasy didn't matter. When the law was laid down, you agreed!

"I want you to stay home from the Masonic

Meeting this week," she added.

This was getting close to the line for Richard, but he'd heard that a couple members had fallen ill after a committee meeting earlier in the week. He wasn't sure what ailed them, but it seemed prudent to accept the possibility that it might be healthier to not attend than to do so, for a couple weeks anyway.

"I'll be using the well for wash water and cooking, but I don't want you using it to drink, Richard," she warned.

"I think you're going a bit overboard on that," Richard offered.

It was a rearguard action and he knew it, but resistance had to be offered if only to lay the ground for future engagements.

"Humor me," Maryanne said with the same menace that Richard remembered from his mother, on an occasion he couldn't quite place. "You can drink all the beer you want instead - as long as it isn't water in that mug," Maryanne continued gesturing to the mug at his place at the table.

It was a huge concession on Maryanne's part. She'd never been much of a supporter of the Grog Shops. It was also a safe offer knowing Richard was not much of a drinker anyway.

"It might be time for you to develop a taste for tea

also," she added. "Remember, Richard! Once Cholera gets into a family it can take away everyone! We can't afford such a mistake. I need your word on that."

Richard again looked up from his plate to see flint in his wife's glare. In Richard's memory stirred a dusty memory of his childhood and a trust broken by his father that never was forgiven. He couldn't quite recall the details, but he knew he'd remember it later.

"Hmmmm!" was all Richard said, but he knew, as did Maryanne, that it was as good as his bond.

*

The table had been cleared. It was because he was home in the evenings as summer mellowed into late Fall, that he fell into carving toys for the children. Maryanne was repairing the pocket of his work trousers adding a leather lining to repair the fabric that had worn through.

"It's your penknife that does it, you know."

"Aye! Ma used to say the same thing," Richard murmured. "But you know, there isn't a knife I've seen that is as strong, sharp, and versatile as this one. It's the envy of the shop. It makes old man Bennis proud every time it comes out of my pocket."

Richard turned the small animal he was carving in his hand to balance the body contours. It was a part of the set that would fill Noah's Ark for Christmas for Sarah. He had soldiers and a toy horse and wagon in mind for John

Harvey.

His carving had become surprisingly enjoyable for him and so portable, he wondered why he hadn't taken up the skill earlier. Well the answer to that was obvious once he thought about it; with the arrival of steel pen nibs at the shop, he had no reason to carry a knife to sharpen quills. But the knife was such a part of his life he'd as soon abandon his family as leave it home. The locking pin that Bennis had so cleverly designed, still held the blade as securely as ever and he'd tempered the steel to hold a razor edge. Hence when the quills disappeared from the desks, and Christmas came over the horizon, Richard had taken up the whittling skill he'd admired in others. Material was abundant. He sorted the firewood box for interesting shapes. And if he was really embarrassed about something that split when he tried to hurry, he could send it along the way it was going when he diverted it in the first place.

He had an artist's eye for proportion and symmetry, but it took a while to pull the shape out of the block of wood that was now his constant companion. In the meantime, the fellows at the shop were sure to let him know their thoughts.

"On which end is the head, Richard?"

"I think that's the first three-legged cow I've seen."

"Does that fly or walk?"

But the good-natured teasing was replaced with a line-up of requests after Richard made a soldier with arms that swung, for Mr. Stanton's new-born son. For Richard, he was delighted with his growing list of carved accomplishments. He now knew how to turn the horse's head just a bit to make the horse seem to be about to move. He found himself seeing with new eyes as he caught flowers nodding, fish jumping after a fly or the family dog bristling at a raccoon.

*

Dear Ma,   October 8, 1834

I am writing to let you know how we are. Our family has grown now that we are well situated here. Sarah will be ten soon and John Harvey is seven, Anna Helena is six, and Mary had her fifth birthday back in April. Helen Price and I have been longtime friends. We are teaching out own children and several others in the neighbourhood. The older children are able to read signs on the street, and the newspapers in the town. We must censor some of the content in the newspapers, it is so violent. We have told you of the strong political powers here that do everything they can to establish a copy of the English aristocracy from which many have come. Standing in opposition to them are many clear and strong voices. One of those voices belongs to William Lyon Mackenzie. We told you earlier how he sued the brigands who broke up his printing press when the Solicitor General refused to bring criminal charges against the thugs. M. refused a settlement and went to a jury who awarded him £625 in damages – enough to set him up for life in opposition! How wonderfully ironic! The comedy has recently continued. We, well the men, I mean, have recently been granted the power to elect representatives to the legislature. M. put his name forward as a candidate and was elected. Since then, he has called for inquiries into the many financial misdeeds of the ruling party. The Family Compact, as they are called here, has expelled him 3 times from the legislature and each time, he is re-elected by his constituents in the ensuing byelection. In the most recent debacle, M. tried twice to take his seat and was only able to finally do so by the order of the Lieutenant Governor Colbourne himself. With each new contest, the language becomes more strident. Richard tries to stay clear in the interest of keeping his job. He says it is the only way to command respect from both sides – by advocating for neither.

The town is growing at a rapid rate. You could tell any on the street in Limerick that there is work for them aplenty here if they can put together the funds for their passage. Men can earn 5s/day at labour. With 3 days' work a week, a man can feed, house, and clothe his family. As you know, the cost of passage for us was more than the money. We think of young John always. Even if they escape the diseases of the voyage, immigrants must still be prepared to battle cholera here. This past summer was the worst in three years. So far, we are safe. Anyone who wants to come here must be prepared to adapt to winter as they have never known it. You can't imagine such cold. Storms lay snow more than knee-deep in the streets. The cold that usually follows makes the snow so cold it squeals underfoot. If it is a moonlight night in such cold, the crystals that form on the snow look as big as dinner plates. It is a magical sight.

Most wagons are replaced by sleds in the winter. Some are quite fashionable. One bundles in thick Buffalo robes to travel any distance in the cold. You learn that it was a good idea to trim your cloak hood with fox fur and take a muff with the fur turned inside for your hands.

Ordinary footwear is inadequate. We all have boots made a size larger than summer boots and then fill the extra space with felt soles and extra wool socks. I am always knitting or mending them. The drying line hung behind the wood stove in the kitchen is constantly in use. We all wear mittens. Mittens are gloves with a single pocket for all your fingers if you can imagine that. By keeping your fingers together, they stay warmer than in gloves. We often wear one pair of mittens inside another. Of course, this makes picking up things clumsy but better clumsy than cold – even frozen. Frozen fingers, or toes, will not heal and must be cut off. In deep winter our bedrooms have layers of frost creeping up the inside of the walls so intense is the cold. You quickly learn the better kinds of wood for fires. Coal or peat is not available here. Logs of well-dried hard wood can burn all night in the stove when it is properly banked. If you use the wrong wood, you wake to a cold kitchen, slow breakfast, and a churlish family.

When the snow melts in the Spring, you should see the streets – rivers they become! Travel between communities is almost impossible till the roads dry out. Travel by ship between ports risks spring storms that are dangerous.

With spring come the hordes of tiny black flies that leave you bleeding from their bites. They are worse in the woods, so bad say some farmers, that deer are driven into their fields to escape. They disappear in a few weeks and then come the mosquitoes. They too, are not found in Limerick. They puncture you and draw blood leaving an itchy spot. The animals suffer badly from them. In the town, we are not so bothered by them except at twilight or before dawn.

Our first frost has come outside York, or Toronto as it is now called, so it is time to get ready for the winter I described. The girls and I are digging up potatoes and carrots and storing them in the small root cellar we made beneath our kitchen floor like the one we had on Mungret Street. Cabbages last well in the small pantry off the kitchen. Our apple crop is a continuing source of joy. Farmers in the market ask to trade cuttings from the trees we brought from Susannah's garden so long ago for their cuttings. There is vigorous interest in crossbreeding trees that can withstand our winters, provide attractive flavours, and last well into the winter without being dried. As I write, Richard and John Harvey are busy stacking the long tall rows of winter's firewood we've arranged for along the back wall of the house where it is out of the rain. We hope this letter finds you as well as we are.

Maryanne

13
CHALLENGE OF FRIENDS

"I can never look at those apple trees without thinking of Susannah. The letter said she'd died peacefully last Fall but every time I see those trees, I feel she is reaching out to us still. She was always looking ahead for us, Richard. It is in her encouragement for us to leave that place, that she gave us her greatest gift," mused Maryanne as she and Richard sat together.

Old blossom petals were drifting about the porch on a swirling breeze in the failing light. They sat on the small back porch looking across their garden and its well-mulched rows of short green sprouts. The yard was now enclosed by a fence of tightly woven willow. Potatoes had just broken the soil this week. Cabbage plants had added two new leaves. The rhubarb was in flower. A stretched string marked where another row of carrots would join those planted weeks before.

The closest row to the string already showed the radishes that marked the row where the carrots would eventually appear. Beside it was the row of carrots already showing four weeks of tops. The family was slowly coming to rest. Sophia, the newborn, was nursing peacefully. Maryanne drew up the collar of her shawl over the baby as she slipped into sleep. The rest of the children were doing writing exercises that Richard had set them at the kitchen table.

"John Harvey is working well at The Gazette," Richard observed, referring to their son. "He shows some of his grandfather's big frame. But I don't want him to be trapped in the trades as I was. I was asking about getting John into the private school where Price sent his Henry. Henry has already graduated and is working as a clerk in the lawyer's office that does lots of work for his Da'. He'll be leaving to go to university in England in the Fall, Harold says. That will guarantee him a place when he returns to practice law here. I'd like John Harvey to be able to look forward to security like that."

Maryanne did not reply.

"I've asked about the entrance requirements for Upper Canada College. Apart from the nine pounds it will cost to have him attend as a day student, he'll have to write an entrance examination. I expect it will be something like the one I wrote to get into the Diocesan School back in Limerick," Richard continued. "What worries me most are the choices I might have to make if J.H. is to be accepted at the College."

Richard was expanding on a continuing dilemma for him, "I fear I may have to disown friends who support Mr. Mackenzie just to ensure John Harvey can enroll. Is that my duty as his father? The tests to be written may not all be John's. It's a question of what I'd do for my children. Can I improve his future?"

Maryanne looked up, "John, for as long as I've known you, you've wanted to belong with those above you. Do you really think that anything you do or say will assure that you will rise above where you were born? Will those you aspire to join ever see past their accent to welcome yours? Be careful whose friendship you trade, for I fear those you seek will not stand by you as your neighbours and family will."

A long silence filled the twilight. "You're probably right. Trading good friends for questionable ones likely won't get me anywhere but a lonely walk home. But can I hope my birth will not taint my son's future? Didn't we leave that in Limerick?" It was a rhetorical question. He carried on almost talking to himself. "Mind you, Mackenzie seems to be sliding ever closer to the Revolutionary vision of our American neighbours. I fear if he does, he'll lose the slender support he is holding here now." Maryanne was silent. "But that makes it easier for me if he walks over the cliff by himself," he thought on the other hand.

By then the insects were becoming a nuisance. "Lots of mosquitoes tonight," Maryanne observed. "There must be a storm coming. They always seem most hungry before it rains." She rose from her rocker, "Time to go in."

Maryanne led them into the kitchen and straight across to

the crib in the corner where she tucked a sleeping Sophia under a light blanket. Richard entered behind her and closed the door before leaning over the kitchen table between the children.

"How are you doing on those exercises?" asked Richard. He was looking over what John Harvey had copied into script from the newspaper when a timid knock came from the front door.

"Who could that be?" asked Maryanne, immediately alarmed at the intrusion at that hour and especially after the talk of Mackenzie.

There was rebellious talk on the streets, and she wanted Richard to have nothing to do with it. Richard scooped up one of the two, lighted lamps from where the children were working and walked to the door and carefully opened the door. A male figure was silhouetted against the fading sunset. Beyond in the gloomy street was a woman and some children tugging at her skirts.

"Yes Sir! How can I help you," asked Richard with authority, holding the lamp high so it would light the man.

"Richard? Richard Watson?" croaked the man at the door as he pulled off his hat and held it in front of his chest.

Richard recognized the voice immediately but could not see the visitor's face. He leaned a little closer to study the lined and stubbled face.

"My God, Sean? Sean O'Connor?" Whispered Richard incredulously as he stared at the scarecrow figure before him, "Is it really you?"

The man could not reply for a spell. He stood there with tears streaming down his face.

Finally clearing his throat, he said with the lilt that Richard had apprenticed with, he said, "Aye, it is me Richard, and my family. We heard about you from the letter your good wife wrote home. We've come to seek our fortune but we're a long way from it now. Could you help us out?"

Richard reached out for the man's shoulder as he said, "Of course, Man!"

But as he touched Sean's shoulder, he felt the bones beneath the jacket. *There is no muscle there at all*, he thought.

"Come in, come in," urged Richard as he drew Sean through the door, "Maryanne, come see. We have friends from Limerick. It's Sean O'Connor and he brings a family."

Richard swung his attention to the huddle in the street. "Come in," he beckoned. "I'm Richard Watson and this is my wife Maryanne." Maryanne was at his shoulder greeting Sean, then turned to the shadows approaching the door.

"Please come in she called. I'm Maryanne Watson."

The women were left in the dark as Richard led Sean toward the kitchen. They bumped together as they followed the men down the short passage to the kitchen.

"I'm Brigitte," said the bundle of hair and tattered clothes in the darkness beside her.

That was all she had time for before they came into the light of the kitchen. Sarah and John Harvey had joined Anna Helena on the other side of the table where they stood silent and wide-eyed.

"John Harvey, Sarah, Anna Helena this is the oldest friend I have. He and his family have come from Limerick. I learned my trade with him," Richard explained.

There was an awkward pause. Maryanne was scrutinizing her guests for sign of sickness and was relieved to find none. But she could smell the stink of the ship rising from their clothes like a fog.

"Are you a printer?" asked John Harvey.

"No, my lad, I'm a printer's assistant. There isn't anything I don't know about printing except reading and setting type. There isn't a press I can't fix. But I can't fix what I don't have and that's why we're here. I was fired from the job I had, the one I kept when your Da' left to come here."

Surprised at his son's boldness, Richard ushered Sean to a chair at the kitchen table as Maryanne did the same for Brigitte.

Brigitte introduced her children, "This is Liam," she said with a hint of pride, in her voice as she tugged the sleeve of her taller child. "He's eight. And this is Clare," she nodded to the child whose thumb was stuck into her mouth to the second knuckle, "She's three."

As if she knew she'd been missed, the bundle in the sling Brigitte carried squirmed and whimpered, "This is Molly, but she is pretty weak," The baby was struggling in her mother's arms.

Maryanne immediately spotted the problem. She locked eyes with Brigitte, "Could I nurse her, do you think," Maryanne offered gently. Tears flowed down Brigitte's cheeks as she nodded.

"Give me a minute," interrupted Maryanne as she turned to the stove where the leftovers of the dinner's stew were still warm in the pot.

She tipped the large simmering kettle into the pot. From the smaller tea kettle, she added hot water to the tea pot with fresh tea. With a dipper, she refilled both kettles from the water bucket on the counter beside the stove and set them back on the stove.

As the tea steeped, she gave a quick stir of the pot measuring the amount with a practiced eye and tossed a few sticks of kindling into the firebox of the stove.

"Can I offer you some tea?" Maryanne asked.

"We're not used to tea," apologized Brigitte.

"Well, here you will learn what a refreshing drink it is," Maryanne said. "It is healthy to drink water that has been boiled. Don't ask me why. Here we are," Maryanne announced as she moved the teapot to a pad on the table. "Sarah, reach me cups for everyone."

Sarah slid past the other children and collected cups from the cupboard. It took two trips to set enough. Maryanne poured a round. As the adults reached for the steaming brew, Sarah pushed two small cups to Liam and Clare.

"Blow it first till it's cool or you'll burn your tongue," Sarah cautioned them. Both children cupped the warm cup and blew the steam off the top then watched as it reformed.

While Sarah was instructing the children, Maryanne opened the back door to the porch. The breeze was stronger now, she noticed. She sniffed. *Rain coming*, she thought. She dragged her rocking chair into the kitchen and over to the corner beside the crib.

"Now let's see if we can make that baby happy," said Maryanne as she sat down; she opened her blouse and held out her arms.

Brigitte lifted the baby from her sling, pulled back the

blanket around the child's face. The baby immediately twisted her face back and forth. Maryanne offered the baby her breast and the child latched on like it was all she knew. A tiny hand struggled free of the blanket and patted Maryanne's breast. In only a few minutes, Molly had emptied what was left from feeding Sophia earlier and Maryanne switched sides.

"That's not much but it's enough for now, little one," Maryanne murmured a few minutes later after baby had emptied the second breast.

She lifted Molly and handed her back to Brigitte who swung the baby to her shoulder for burping.

"She got more than I have, I fear," Brigitte sniffed.

"We can give her some more during the night," Maryanne said in return. "She can nurse a little more often and in smaller amounts and that will increase my supply to help yours."

"Thank you," whispered Brigitte as she closed her eyes sending another stream of tears down her cheeks.

The whole table had been engrossed in the drama with the baby but as Molly gave a healthy burp, everyone seemed to return to blowing the steam off their tea.

Maryanne fastened her blouse and stood, "Did you have supper?" she asked.

The children bowed over the remains of their tea.

Brigitte turned her face into the bundle at her shoulder.

Sean looked up, "Not since night before last," he said.

"Well, you came to the right spot, you did. But this meal will be the longest you will remember. When you've not been eating much, you will get sick if you eat a lot at once. You can have all the bowls the pot holds, but only a bit at a time. Let me start you with a bit now. Anna Helena, some bowls and spoons please."

Maryanne swung back to the stove and added more hot water from the kettle to the pot before refilling the kettle again. Anna Helena had brought the bowls to the stove where she followed her mother's example and quarter-filled them. John stepped over and handed the bowls back to the table. While the children served the soup, Maryanne stepped to the wooden box in which the three loaves of sourdough bread she'd baked that morning were stored. She placed a large loaf on a platter at hand and quickly cut it into a dozen pieces then and brought it to the table. The children stared at Brigitte waiting for a nod before they picked up their spoons and lunged into their bowls.

"Slowly," Brigitte said sharply, and the children cut to half-speed. It took no time to finish the half dozen spoonsful.

"Same for the bread," Maryanne cautioned. She lifted a slice for each guest with the tip of the knife, "Nibble slowly," she said. "Richard, Sarah, John Harvey, would you like some more tea?" Maryanne asked to deflect attention.

The guests had finished two small servings each when Maryanne caught Richard's eye. Words passed silently in the glance.

"Before you eat more, and I expect you to do so, it is time to set up some sleeping space for you. John Harvey, Sarah, bring down the winter blankets and quilts to the parlour. Mary, you show the children where the outhouse is. Here, take the lantern."

"Ooh no," protested Sean. "We didn't mean to do more than come to find you. You've been too generous already. We should be on our way." He was half standing when Richard put a restraining hand on his shoulder.

"Sean, you are my oldest friend and you stood by me many times at your cost. I never was able to repay your friendship though I wanted to so often. Please, sit. Stay till we can find you a job and some place to live. Besides, how would it look to send a friend into the street with a storm coming. It is your duty to stay and save my reputation with the neighbours."

"You do have a way with words Richard Watson, I'll say that," and then after a pause, "Thank you. We'd be most grateful."

Both families rose from the table to go to the parlour where blankets were spread to make mattresses before they all returned to the kitchen for more soup and bread.

Thunder grumbled in the distance.

Maryanne had cleaned up the dishes and the O'Connors were bedded down when the first lightning flash lit up the room. A suppressed scream came from the parlour. *Sounds like Clare,* thought Maryanne. She was about to pick up the lamp and go up to bed when she remembered. *Better get more sourdough started*, she thought. She got out three extra bowls, poured the milk and flour into each and added three large spoonsful of starter to each. She checked over her shoulder to be sure she was alone in the kitchen before reaching up to take down her pot of maple syrup. Quickly she added two large spoons of syrup to each bowl and stirred it vigorously to hide her secret. Each bowl was covered with a green gingham towel and silently returned to the high shelf where it would rise in time for baking tomorrow. Then she went up to bed.

*

After a quick breakfast of oatmeal cakes, cheese and weak beer, Richard left with Sean and John Harvey before dawn. They were headed for Harold Price's latest building project. All were carrying small pails with lids that slipped down halfway inside before jamming on the sides to keep the double ladle of barley-thickened soup below from slopping out. Above the lid was an empty space where Maryanne had placed a spoon, tin cup and half loaf of sourdough bread fresh from the oven. The bread was sliced crossways and filled with a dollop of butter then wrapped in a green gingham towel for Sean, red for her own men.

As they approached the building site, Richard recognized George Crawford, the foreman, from the Masonic Hall where George had been a recent initiate. George saw them coming. He left the carpenters he'd been instructing and came towards Richard.

"Richard! Good Morning! Good to see you, sir. And John." He nodded to the lad.

"And you also, George. Let me introduce a friend from Limerick. George Crawford, meet Sean O'Connor."

Though they stepped forward to shake hands, the religion in each name signaled to each how far apart they really were.

"Sean and I worked together in Limerick. He did me many favours. He's a good man and he needs a job. What could he do for you now?"

George was used to appraising men on sight. He could see the threadbare clothes, the scrawny arms sticking from the tattered coat sleeves. He knew this man had starved for months. But none of that showed on his weathered face.

"As it happens, I was looking for someone to help young James there. He's to pick up some lumber at the mill and needs an extra hand. Sean is it?"

"Yes sir."

"Could you do that to start the day?"

"Yes sir! With pleasure, sir!"

"Good. That's where you'll begin. We pay five shillings six pence a day; for the first week, you're paid at the end of each day. After that, men are paid on Friday night if you are kept on. Is that agreeable?"

To Sean, the words were a Song of Salvation, but his face was earnest, and eyes fixed on the foreman.

"That sounds fine sir."

"We work till dark; we'll see you here at first light if you're to last the week."

"I'll be here sir."

"Good." The men shook hands on the arrangement.

"Put your lunch pail by the fire there with the others and join James."

"James," George called. The lad approached. "Take Sean to help you! Show him the sights on the way. I expect you back, fully loaded by mid-morning. Don't forget to get a list of what the mill sends with you or I'll have your hide."

"I'll leave you then," said Richard to Sean. "You can find your way home later."

"I can!" He shook Richard's hand and couldn't help smiling.

As Sean turned for the wagon with James, Richard shook George's hand. Their eyes met. Richard recognized the light duty; Sean had been given and his smile and nod was all the recognition George needed. Richard would buy him a drink next week.

"Thanks," Richard said. "Now young fellow let's be off," Richard said to John Harvey and he picked up the pace as they walked, lunch pails swinging, to the office of The Upper Canada Gazette.

14

THE SORORITY

Maryanne and Brigitte had finished feeding the children after the men had left with Sean to get him a job. The women cleaned up the dishes then Maryanne waved Brigitte to a chair. Maryanne smoothed down her apron and set a fresh mug of tea and some cheese before Brigitte. They needed to plan the rest of the day. The children had been sent to the garden to play with the chickens.

"It's as much as your life is worth to step on a row of plants," Maryanne had scowled before sending them out into the fresh and sunny air. "Run on the paths only! Sarah, Anna, make sure they do! Mary, you lead the way around the garden to show where the paths are."

"Yes Ma," came a chorus! The assurance was lost in the scrape of bench and chairs as the children bolted out the door. Molly nursed from both mothers. She burped gently then sat on Brigitte's knee facing the table bright-eyed and looking everywhere.

"You need to eat all of that to get your milk back," Maryanne said as she nudged the plate.

Brigitte took another chunk of bread from the plate and inhaled the aroma before she took a bite, "I never tasted bread as wonderful as this. How do you do it?"

Maryanne took a crumb, sampled it with professional care as she looked at the ceiling.

"I think it tastes like it always does," she said reflectively, but she was secretly proud of her product.

"Well it is sweeter than mine," stated Brigitte flatly. "Will you show me what you do?"

"Maybe later."

When she had finished the last crumb, Brigitte whispered with downcast eyes, "I'll never be able to thank you enough."

As she raised her eyes, she found herself looking into Maryanne's steady eyes.

"I expect you will, if you help the next person," Maryanne said. "I'm only passing on what Helen Price did for me. You're part of the sisterhood now."

Brigitte felt elation she had never known, "So it's the Mothers of Mercy, are we?" Brigitte burst out with a guffaw. "You'll be talking about Holy Orders next!"

And the two women laughed and laughed, one for joy, the other for relief.

When they finally caught their breath, Maryanne stood and said, "If I remember my own arrival here, the first thing I wanted was to be free of the smell of that ship."

Brigitte's eyes shot to the ceiling and her gasp told Maryanne it was a shared feeling.

"So, I suggest we hang up a curtain on the porch around the tub we use for bathing, and you can start with the children. There's lots of water in the rain barrel from the storm last night but I'll tell you, it will be cold. There's warm water for Molly."

Maryanne walked to the shelf by the kitchen door to the porch, "Here's some soap." Maryanne handed her a palm-sized block of creamy-brown soap, and, plucking a sheet from the back of her chair. "You can dry off with this."

Turning the soap in her hand, Brigitte mused to herself, "This looks good enough to eat."

Without a pause, Maryanne stepped back towards the crib in the corner where she had stacked clothes she'd brought down before breakfast.

"You can dress the children in these. I think they'll fit. My children have outgrown them, but I think they might fit yours. Brigitte recognized the mended garments for what they were. She noted separate clothes for herself at the bottom of the pile and closed her eyes in thanks. All they had is what the stood in. It was the two lengths of green ribbon that peaked out from under the dress, that sent her eyes back to Maryanne's.

"For your hair and Clare's," Maryanne said with a smile.

"You are just a saint," laughed Brigitte.

The women had walked out onto the back porch where Maryanne looped up cords that hung on nails at head height, to similar nails on the opposite posts. She tossed sheets over the three cords to curtain off an enclosure against the wall around an empty half-barrel, set with one edge overlapping the edge of the porch floor. A bench, pail, dipper and comb completed the necessities.

"When we're done bathing, I can tap out that bung at the bottom and drain the water into pails to water the garden," Maryanne explained. "There is fresh water for you and warm water for the baby," she reminded Brigitte. "Now I'll bring some water from the rain barrels for the tub," offered Maryanne.

She picked up a bucket and walked towards the corner of the house. "All right then," she said when she returned. "Pile all the clothes you're wearing in the wash tub over there," Maryanne pointed to a second half barrel with a washboard sticking out of it on the porch behind her, "and we'll wash them up after everyone is clean. Then we'll go to the market so I can show you where to buy things. We'll also stop by some rooming houses I know to see if we can find you a place to call your own."

While Brigitte bathed the children and herself, Maryanne summoned the children to help her in the garden.

"Sarah, you and Anna Helena get buckets and fill them with mulch from those rotted leaves in the corner," she pointed towards the pile beside the outhouse at the foot of the garden, "and bring them back here."

The girls headed to the porch where two small buckets were upended.

"Now watch Mary, these carrot seeds as so small, and you have to put them three fingers-space apart." She started to drop a pinch of seeds one or two at a time, into a groove she'd made with her finger beneath the string that stretched down the row. "You put one of those radish seeds in the grove every two hands apart," she directed Mary.

With the fixation of a young child, Mary did as she was bid. They had planted about six feet of row when the other girls returned with half full buckets of rotted leaves. Mary stuck a twig vertically into the soil to mark how far she'd planted then turned to the girls.

"Watch now!" She directed the girls, "We push the edges of the groove over on the seeds, so they are buried with no more than a finger's width of soil and pat it down gently. Good night seeds," she said, for Mary's benefit, "Sleep well."

Everyone took a piece of the row and covered the seeds.

"Your mulch is next, girls. I want a layer this wide,' she placed her hand across the row, "From fingertip to wrist lightly along on top of the seeds. This will keep the rain from beating the seeds out of the ground and the birds from finding them. You start on this section," she indicated the part they had just planted. "Mind you leave my marker, so I know where to start planting again. Mary, we'll go to the other end of the row to plant while Saran and Anna Helena do their part. Then trade places so we're not in each other's way."

From the porch the shivers and complaints of cold water baths was plainly coming to an end. Scrubbed faces and wet hair popped from behind the curtains in fresh clothes. Maryanne smiled as Liam and Clare joined them to watch the process. Brigitte stepped from behind the curtain cinching up the belt that secured Maryanne's old skirt.

"I have the waist I had as a bride," she joked ruefully.

She picked up the fresh apron that Maryanne had left outside the curtain on a nail then reached back for the knitted black shawl Maryanne had set out as a sling for Molly. She knotted the shawl as needed and slipped it over her shoulder then sat on the edge of the porch to pick up her baby laying there. Lulled by the warm bath and another small feeding, the baby drifted to sleep. Brigitte stowed the baby in her sling, picked up the soap and came over to sort the laundry, rolling up her sleeves as she came.

"My how nicely it smells," she mused.

"Now if you stand over here," Maryanne drew her to the ground beside the porch. "When the tub is on the porch just those two steps higher, and you're standing down here, it's a whole lot easier on your back, I've found."

Brigitte tossed the first dirty clothes into the water as Maryanne pulled down the curtains and folded them onto the bench.

"I've never met anyone as organized as you are," Brigitte said, shaking her head.

"Ladies and gentlemen," Maryanne announced with a huckster's cry to the children who had just finished mulching the newly planted carrots. "Step this way please for a sight never seen by human eyes. Bring your pail."

Liam and Clare gathered curiously with widened eyes. Sarah and Anna Helena knew what was coming and hung back. Mary stood in front of the group with Clare. Maryanne dropped a pail beneath the bunghole in the bottom of the barrel of bathwater where the barrel stuck out beyond the porch floor. She plunged her bare arm into the grubby bath water and wiggled it.

With a flourish of her other hand, she shouted, "Abra Kadabrah," and immediately water started to flow out of the hole in the bottom of the tub and into the pail. Clare's mouth dropped open and she squealed with laughter. Liam tossed his head with mature disdain. The pail was almost filled.

"Clare, tell the enchanted water to stop. Say *Water STOP!* And wave your hand," Maryanne said.

Clare's squeaky voice shouted the spell, and immediately the water stopped. Clare looked at her hand and then at the full pail. Pulling her hand from the tub, and drying it on her apron, Maryanne picked up the dipper beside the tub and carried the pail of water to the row of newly-planted seeds followed like she was the Pied Piper, except for Sarah, who had joined Brigitte with fresh rain water for rinsing.

"Stand back so you don't step on the mulch. I want you all to take turns watering the seeds. Take a dipper from the bucket and pour it down the row just at the edge of the mulch, like this," and she showed them all. "Anna Helena, you will be in charge to be sure everyone gets a turn. Show everyone how to do it right."

Anna proudly demonstrated her skill.

"Come back for more water when that is done."

Maryanne left the children pushing to inspect each other's performance. Clare was splashing her hand in the water. When Maryanne returned to the porch, Sarah had rinsed the first clothes and together the two of them had wrung them out.

"Hang those light ones on the line," she pointed her chin to where the curtains had been, "And I'll hang this shawl on the fence."

The sun was rising towards mid-morning when the women were headed down the street to do the day's shopping.

*

"I can't believe it. Less than a day ago we were starving and dirty enough to drive away pigs. And here I am with a full belly, a happy baby, and smelling like a rose. If I live to be a hundred, I can never forget this day! You are truly a blessing, Maryanne Watson. It is a miracle I'm in!" Brigitte laugh matched the sunshine.

"It's what we do," Brigitte. We work miracles," Maryanne replied with that huckster's wave of her hand, "Abra Kadabrah," she shouted! And they strode with shopping baskets on arms and children at hand, towards the market.

As they approached the market, Brigitte turned to her children, "Clare, take Liam's hand." Clare's other thumb was stuck comfortably in her mouth. "Liam, don't let her go."

Maryanne stepped across the street with authority and head high into the first aisle. She ignored men behind the first three tables and stopped at the next.

"Mrs. Jerome, I need five pounds of flour, please," and handed over a bag of tightly woven cotton. She turned back to Brigitte.

"When you buy a large bag of flour in the Fall, you save the bags to make smaller ones because they are really tight cloth and do for all sorts of things."

Madame Jerome used a large wooden scoop to move the brownish whole-wheat flour into Maryanne's bag on the scale till it balanced the sliding weight set as she'd asked, then added another part scoop.

"That's for the bag's weight," the lady said as she looked at Brigitte, recognizing her as a new face and potential customer.

"Have you some corn meal, and ground oats?" asked Maryanne, "Five of oats if you have them, two of corn?"

"We have both, but this will be the last week for corn meal till the new crop's in," Mrs. Jerome replied.

"Better make it four pounds of corn meal then," as Maryanne passed over two more bags.

The merchant made sure Brigitte saw she added the bag's weight and a bit more to the scales before she tied each bag with twine and handed them back. Maryanne passed over coins she withdrew from a purse drawn from the pocket of her skirt but secured by a long tether to her belt.

"That was generous of her," Brigitte commented quietly as they walked away.

"Well, I like that, and I know she doesn't add sand to her flour like those others do," Maryanne whispered back. "They say it's the grit from the grindstones, but I know grit from sand any day."

They walked on toward the meat vendors. Sausages and ham were on display. Maryanne recognized venison and pointed out the difference in fat to Brigitte. Beef was further on. After surveying what was on offer, Maryanne was about to choose sausages when she asked Brigitte,

"Does your family like sausages?"

"Maryanne, I don't remember the last time we had them. We ate them a long time ago, but that was like in a dream."

"Three and a half pounds, please," she said to Mr. Hardy behind the table.

He counted out fourteen links and cut them from the circle on the counter then placed them in the scale, "That's closer to three and three quarters ma'am."

"Fine," said Maryanne, but when her change came back, Brigitte noted that she'd been charged for the three and a half pounds she'd asked for.

"Sarah, will you carry that in your basket please?"

Sarah handed over her basket for Hardy to tuck in the paper-wrapped bundle.

"Now some potatoes," Maryanne said. She caught Brigitte's closed eyes and small moan. Immediately, Maryanne looked at her with concern, "Are you all right?"

Brigitte had stopped dead in the midst of the stream of customers. She looked up to keep tears from her eyes.

"Maryanne, you have no idea what it's like to open a pit of potatoes as you have for your whole life and see nothing but black goo. And then you go to the next one, and it's the same. You know you and your children will be starving before next week..." She breathed deeply a couple times, "I'll be all right now."

They walked along the aisle to a small table of potatoes. Full sacks stood beside.

"Good Morning Mrs. Brooks," she said to the matronly woman behind the table. "I'm here with a guest from the land of potatoes. Have you anything for us today?"

"They're a bit sprouted but I've been keeping them in our ice pit. They'll eat well enough," replied Brooks

"Could we have fifteen?" Maryanne asked.

"Brigitte could you carry those?"

"I think so," Brigitte said.

She handed over her basket for loading. They were counted out by Mrs. Brooks and little Mary was asked to count them as well. The other mother humoured the recount by the child as Maryanne paid for them. Brigitte stroked the smooth dusty skin and sucked in the moisture in her mouth. She lowered the basket so Clare could see in.

"Remember what those are, Clare?"

"Tato's," said the child as she took her thumb out of her mouth.

"Let's walk past the fishmongers," Maryanne guided the entourage toward the tables at the end of the aisle. The smell of wet fish surrounded them. "We have good fish here, but you may not recognize them." Maryanne pointed out the various kinds, some still flopping in the trays, "Trout is really easy to fillet. Or eat. The meat comes off the bones easily. That one with the big teeth is a pike. Tastes well but the bones are all shaped like a 'Y' so you must eat it slowly to keep from getting bones stuck in your throat. These are salmon. Unless you are feeding an army, you only buy a piece. But it is delicious. You can preserve it by smoking it. Or perhaps Mr. Weedrick here," she nodded to the man in front of her, "will do it for you in his smoke house."

Weedrick took the cue to pick up a chunk of smoked salmon, "Care to try a sample?" The small bite quickly became six as each child expected a taste.

"I don't like it," declared Clare.

"Let me look after that piece for you," said Brigitte and it disappeared between Brigitte's teeth before Clare could draw breath to reconsider.

They left the market and took a path through vacant lots towards home. Along the way, three rooming houses had no room but suggested that some of their boarders would be headed out within the week to farms near Hamilton and London. They were told to check each day.

Maryanne renewed the invitation to stay with them as long as they needed to. The vacant lots had a fine crop of flowers and Maryanne showed Brigitte how to pick the young green leaves to add to stews and soups for flavour. They arrived home and Maryanne immediately offered tea as she stuffed kindling into the coals in the firebox and moved the tea kettle up to the front of the stovetop. It was still hot from breakfast.

"Water would do," suggested Brigitte.

"I've found we stay healthy when we drink tea or weak beer," Maryanne reminded her. "Let's wait a few minutes for the kettle to boil and put away this food in the meantime."

15
OH, SEAN! YOU'VE DONE IT!

Sean arrived back at the Watson's as the twilight was fading. He was bone weary but there was a smile on his face that lit up the room. He banged his closed hand on the kitchen table in front of Brigitte, flipped it over, opened it up and lifted it clear. Five shillings and six pence glowed softly in the lamplight.

"Oh Sean! You've done it!" Brigitte clasped his hand and kissed it, tears streaking her face again. For a moment, she was surprised she had any tears left. She looked into the eyes of her happy man and pressed his hand to her cheek. The rest had already eaten earlier – lightly, expecting to join Sean when he came it. Richard had set Sarah, Anna Helena, and Mary to more writing exercises. Liam and Clare were at the other end of the table with John Harvey and the wooden alphabet blocks naming letters as John pointed to them and then arranging them to make everyone's name.

Brigitte broke the moment by standing and declaring that Sean had one more duty before dinner, "To the porch, bathe and come in clean before you get a bite. There are clean clothes on the bench, and hot water to take the chill off the water in the tub. Go now," she ordered pointing towards the back door.

"Too much bathing is unhealthy you know," Sean quipped as he stood back from the table and arched his back, "but if a bath a year will keep the peace." He gave a theatrical sigh. Then leaned forward to slide all the coins in front of Richard who was reading.

Richard didn't touch them only smiled as he looked up, "Get washed, you lout so you can join we civilized people."

Brigitte boosted the larger of the two kettles brimming with hot water from the stove out to the porch. They all could hear the water pouring into the tub and then the suppressed laughs, splashing and groaning of private moments that followed. Maryanne noisily stoked the fire in the stove and banged her large frying pan with unaccustomed zeal as she set sausages to fry.
They had finished the sausages and potatoes. The plates had been moved away and the children shooed to bed before Richard pushed the coins that had sat on the table all meal, back towards Sean.

"You earned these if any man did, today and these were the last test that George Crawford set you today." Richard said as he pointed with his chin to the coins.

"Does the job never end?" groaned Sean in mock agony. "I thought I was done for the day when I walked in and I haven't stopped working since!" He pushed the coins closer towards Richard.

"Those are surely yours and much more for taking us in and putting us all in new clothes." He was uncomfortable about receiving charity.

"Those clothes will hardly last till you need others. You are exaggerating in your usual Irish way," Richard smiled, "And as for taking you in, what are friends for?"

There was an awkward pause as all the adults focused on the coins glowing dully beside the teapot.

"Let me tell you about the test Crawford has set you. It's not over yet. He paid you knowing it is just good business. He can't get nearly enough good men to finish those buildings and make more money on the next set. Crawford can test them on the job, but he gives every new man his pay at nightfall to see if he'll show up next morning sober instead of hung over or not at all. Those who show up, he tests with more money the next night. It's' like the Bible. Three times, the Lord was tested. It's rope to see if you'll hang yourself." Richard elaborated.

"I'm not sure if I should feel dead or divine already," joked Sean.

Richard pressed on, "You all need the money," Richard's wave towards the other room ended with Brigitte, "to find lodging, buy food and just keep standing after a day's work. We're one of the props, that's all, and to see you finish the week, is our reward. As I said, I owe you a lot. What has happened here, is small repayment indeed. Besides, it is far too proud of you to think that is your money. It properly belongs to Brigitte."

"Rightly said," Maryanne added.

She moved the coins to Brigitte and took a fresh handkerchief from where she'd hidden it on the chair beside her. Without another word, she knotted the money into the corner of the handkerchief, pulled Brigitte's hand toward her, and placed the cloth in her palm.

"That weathered old thing can feel as dead as he wants," Brigitte said as she nodded towards Sean. "I'm feeling divine." With a long look at Maryanne then Richard she said with all the conviction she had, "We will make good here. Thank-you."

Sean was almost to the door to the Parlour when he turned.

"As long as I've got you feeling generous Richard, would you teach us all to read and write?"

"Too late," Richard replied over his shoulder. "The rest of your family are a city block ahead of you and will be dragging you to your lessons to-morrow before you eat dinner. Think on that tomorrow if you aren't tired enough. Now get to bed. The sun rises early."

16
JAIL

"Carfrae was shot in that skirmish of rebels up at Montgomery's tavern!" Shouted Richard as he burst into the office of The Upper Canada Gazette.

Robert Stanton was already at this office door with a stern look on his face. He looked up from a letter in his hand.

"Watson," he said without preamble, "I want you to print up a poster offering a reward for the apprehension of Mr. William Lyon Mackenzie and his rebel leaders – one thousand pounds for Mackenzie and five hundred pounds for the others!"

Richard stopped dead in his tracks and stared wide-eyed at Stanton.

"I have here, over the seal of the Lieutenant Governor himself, an order to that effect," continued Stanton. "I want that poster on the street before you leave to-day, Watson."

"May I see the letter, Sir," Richard mumbled.

Richard was stunned by the size of the rewards. That sort of money was a life-long pension that would keep any family in comfort. He flashed back to his youth in Limerick when similar rewards for rebels or their weapons were shouted out in the parade square of Limerick Castle. He recalled the silent response, hundreds strong, from his neighbours facing the regiment and its gold-braided Colonel. He remembered that not one person claimed the reward. Would it be the same here? Would your barn ever be safe if you turned in any one of them?

The puddles of melted snow dripping from his boots pooled beneath Richard's bench as he locked the woodcut of the Royal Seal in the center at the top of the printing frame. He was not going to entrust this to anyone else. Besides if he had to write it out first, it would slow the whole process down.

No, better drop the Crest down a bit and put the date above. Yes. That frames the Seal nicely. A Proclamation, he thought. *No, shorten that 'Proclamation'- in 36 point. I'll use the same for the reward down below. It gives balance to the page and emphasizes the amount. The heavy lines will give gravity and authority.*

Richard's hands flew above the trays of type, plucking letters up with unconscious speed that always amazed those that watched him. How did he know where the letters were? How did he get them flawlessly right side up?

Ten-point type, **"Let every man now do his duty…"**

Richard slid the letters into the rack faster than most could write. Second line in eight-point type: Keep the focus on the first line. Keep Peace, Order and Good Government at the top of everyone's mind by the words he chose.

Back to ten point: "**Be vigilant, patient and active – leave punishment to the Laws ...**" Make that stand out. Use a short paragraph. And then the crash of thirty-six-point blackness surrounded by white.

'One thousand Pounds'

Back to eight point: "To anyone who will apprehend and deliver up to Justice...," eight point capitals for his name WILLIAM LYON MACKENZIE; "lower case," "and'" capitals again "FIVE HUNDRED POUNDS to any one – same print size ... DAVID GIBSON...SAMUEL LOUNT...JESSE LLOYD...or SILAS FLETCHER and a free pardon...to any of their accomplices..."
ten point... "The only thing that remains to be done, is to find them, and arrest them."

Please God, may they have already escaped, thought Richard to himself as he set the last line. Capitals, ten point; "R. STANTON, Printer to the QUEEN'S Most Excellent Majesty" Richard tapped the last letters and lead lines into place and locked up the frame. He would have to run a test piece of course, but he knew it would be correct.

"Ian, print off a test piece please."

It was back to Richard in minutes. Ian didn't place it on the press for this test. He just rolled a light layer of ink onto the type and then pressed the paper against it with another light roller. Ian brought it back holding the edges to keep the ink from smearing.

"Is this satisfactory?" Asked Richard as he laid the sample on the clean counter and called Stanton from his office. "Careful of your sleeves sir. The ink is still wet."

Reflexively, Stanton pulled up the ruffled cuffs of his white shirt and bent forward. His eyes had been giving him trouble lately. As soon as Richard saw his squint, he handed Stanton the magnifying glass.

"Hmmm," grunted The Queen's Printer.

Richard had already left for the other room while Stanton scanned the text, to instruct the men on which paper to use and what ink. They would need the India ink base this time. It would dry quickly and not run in the weather because these would be nailed outdoors to trees, and posts as well as every wall in town. It would be more difficult to clean off the type later, but that's what labourers were for.

When he returned to the counter, Stanton called his attention to the absence of the year in the bottom corner.

"I set it at the top sir," Richard said pointing upward. Stanton flushed at missing it.

"In that position, it gives balance to the page and

frames the Royal Seal as it should," Richard offered. "I think this has the balance and presentation that gives it authority sir."

"Agreed, Watson," He looked at the page one last time. "Go to press."

"Ian!" Richard called, "As soon as you have one hundred printed, send John Harvey out with one of the other men to tack one on every post on Front Street east of Yonge. When the next hundred are done, you take them yourself and go west from Yonge on Front. I expect you back in no more than an hour. It will be dark by then."

*

It was far past dark when Richard and John Harvey finally left The Gazette offices.

"Have you got the lunch pails?" Richard asked as the left.

John Harvey held them up, "Yes sir," and passed his pail to Richard after Richard had locked the door.

It took a while for their eyes to adjust to the pale moonlight. As they walked, John Harvey found that his pail made a small squeak as he swung it. He changed the swing to see if he could tease out a different sound.

Richard interrupted his preoccupation by saying, "When revolt is in the air, it's a time to beware!"

"You should be a poet, Da'," quipped John.

There was just no putting this kid down, thought Richard.

"Hummph," muttered Richard in response. They walked a few minutes in silence before Richard said, "You should know that people use even the thought of revolt to settles scores or right injustices they imagine. It is not a time to be looking for reason. That is one of the memories I carry from Limerick," Richard replied, and he picked up the pace.

They were about halfway home when a group of men bearing torches came round a corner two streets ahead and started walking towards them.

"I don't like the look of this," Richard muttered to his son as they moved to the side of the road. They took a few steps further. "Guns," he whispered as he saw the glint off a rifle barrel. Richard hip bumped his son into the cleft between two houses.

"Hide," he hissed. His tone brooked no debate. John immediately ducked down behind some wooden crates in the lane between the houses. Richard walked on without breaking stride.

"Here's one," shouted someone in the group.

"Grab him," said someone else.

The group surrounded Richard and thrust the sputtering torches towards him. Richard couldn't see for the flames.

"Who are you and what are you doing out after curfew?" Demanded a voice heavy with theatrical authority.

"I didn't know there was a curfew," said Richard levelly. "But I've been at work printing up the Wanted Poster for William MacKenzie." He reached in his pocket for a copy that was slightly smeared and so not sent out. "Here," he offered. It was snatched from his hand.

"He's been tearing them down," accused a voice.

"Mackenzie's a printer. This is one of his traitorous friends," came another voice behind Richard. A rifle butt hit him in the shoulders. He dropped his lunch pail, and as he bent to pick it up, a boot stomped on it.

"Is that a weapon you carry?" Came another voice behind him and he was jerked sideways by a hand grabbing his collar.

"Who is your officer," Richard asked as he staggered erect holding his fear and temper in check.

"That's Who is your officer, SIR," Another voice shouted.

Richard caught the smell of liquor, "Yes sir! Who is your officer, sir?" Richard repeated, voice and eyes lowered.

"It's Captain MacLean, and don't you forget it." Another shove came from behind pushing him towards the silent man in front of him.

Richard looked up. He knew all the officers in the militia and of the regular forces at the fort. This was not one of them. The man was standing with the wrinkled poster in his hand. It was obvious he couldn't read it. Richard could feel the fear in his belly. What happened in the next few minutes could save his life.

"I don't recognize you, so I guess you must have been deputized because of the fight at Montgomery's Tavern this morning. They need every good man they can get. You can see from the poster that the government wants you to leave punishment to the Law. See it there, just above the reward?" Richard pointed slightly blessing the inspiration that had him put that line in place. "I think it would look good on your record if you brought me in for questioning, Captain." Richard paused for a breath. "There isn't a window on the street that doesn't have someone watching you do your duty and protect them as you were commissioned." Richard looked along the houses, hoping what he said, was so. "So, it is important to come out of this proudly… sir. You could take me to the gaol for safekeeping till you reported to you superior."

"He knows about the fight. He's one of them that escaped," shouted that same alcoholic breath behind him.

"Bind the man," ordered MacLean.

A rope snaked around Richard's wrists tying them behind and another whack with an axe handle to the side of his head stunned him.

"Take him to the gaol," ordered MacLean, and the mob set off in that direction.

They had disappeared before John Harvey crept from his hiding place, picked up the crushed lunch pail in the roadway, and dashed for home.

*

The gaol reeked! It was the ship he'd arrived in all over again. There was a stinking half-filled bucket in the corner of the cell, and the smell of vomit rose from an unconscious man along the back wall. The smell of nervous sweat stirred everything together. Richard's charge was recorded in the Register at the desk as 'Treason' beside his name before he was pushed into a cell crowded with the night's collection. He was getting his bearings, still a bit woozy from the smack on his head. Everyone in the cell had turned to see who the new arrival was.

"Mr. Watson?" asked a voice.

"Is that you, Ian?" Richard asked as he recognized the labourer from The Gazette.

"The same," came the reply as Ian shouldered his way to a place beside Richard. "I see they caught you too. I'd just finished posting the last of the posters you gave me and was going home as you said when this bunch of thugs grabbed me. I thought they was going to beat me to death."

"Is there anyone else you know here?" asked Richard.

"Yes. John Lumsden is over there with a couple of his mates from the Colonial office."

"Where?" Richard asked, and Ian dragged him through the protesting muddle to where Lumsden and the two workers from his office were crowded together.

"They dragged us out of the office at pistol point just after mid-day," Lumsden said. "I guess Mackenzie was in that fight up Yonge St. and because we were at work, we were suspect. Tarred with the same brush we were. What about you?" he asked Richard.

"They're just vigilantes," Richard said. "But when they're liquored up and carry weapons, it's best not to ask too many questions." Richard related his tale and his relief that he'd gotten to the safety of the gaol with only a lump and a bloody scalp. "John was hiding and would have seen it all," Richard continued in a whisper. "He's told his Ma' by now. She'll tell Stanton and he'll be here in the morning to get us out. I'll speak for you and your helpers John."

*

Everyone in the Masonic Hall was shocked at the announcement preceding the regular meeting, of Thomas Carfrae's death that afternoon. He had been ailing, they all knew. His heart problems had been the reason he had stepped down from his position as Grand master of the Lodge even before he was wounded back in 1838. It was hard to take in the loss of such a powerful leader.

"He died of a heart seizure as he was walking home," said his son. That set off another wave of conversation that was hard to overcome in order that the meeting should begin.

*

Richard and Maryanne attended the wake at the Carfrae residence two days later. It was at that gathering that the secretary to Rev. Strachan himself, informed Richard that John Harvey had been accepted into Upper Canada College in the Fall.

17
ESTABLISHED

"This letter says you failed your final exams," Richard said as he waved it at John Harvey, "A whole year shot and enough money to feed a family. Have you an explanation?"

John Harvey, as any fourteen-year-old could only hang his head in shame. He was browbeaten yet again, and it was always about school. When he was working at The Gazette, he and his Da' never had confrontations like this. Thinking back to that memorable night in the street when he and his Da' were caught by the mob and arrested.

He raised his eyes to look into his father's and said, "Do you remember the night the mob caught us on the street?"

As though I could forget, Richard thought. But he said nothing, only waited for John Harvey to continue.

"You didn't raise a finger when they beat and humiliated you. I can't fight back now, as you could not then. There are too many standing against me." John was going for broke now. He was flushed and spit was flying from his mouth as he shouted on, "I can spell, and write and compose as well as the best, but the other students have never done a day's work in their lives. They do everything to obstruct me because I have. When I go to the library to get a book I need, it has been taken out. If I find the book when it is returned, the pages I need are sometimes torn out. Last spring, the teacher accused me of tearing out the pages when he found them folded in my assignment. That's for starters."

He'd risen from the table and was pacing the kitchen. "The geometry, and surveying and other mathematics lessons are a closed book to me. It's like I haven't got the map everyone else seems to have. So, I spend all the time I have just to make middle marks there and other subjects suffer." He paused, a bit out of breath, and sat again, "I can't tell you about food that gets tipped on me at lunch, by accident of course. If I have only one social sleight a day it has been a good one. I feel like oil on water." John suddenly stopped his head down and eyes firmly fixed on the table. He was blinking frantically so his father would only see dry eyes.

The silence was absolute.

"Is it a couple of bullies?" Richard asked after a few moments.

The story poured out, "I was delivering appointment cards and stationery to the Stevens legal office a few years back."

Richard nodded. He knew the name and address well.

"I stood inside the door waiting to be recognized. The men were talking, and one was taking off a bandage from the bridge of the nose of an apprentice. *Will it be healed up for your call to the bar ceremony? One clerk asked. It damn well better be, was the nasal reply as the victim patted his badly squashed nose. I'm going to get that bugger at Mackenzie's office if it's the last thing I do, he continued. Lumsden is his name. I'm going to find him and make him suffer like he never has before.*

"That's when they noticed me."

What do you want, boy? he shouted.

"He scared me. I held out the package. I asked his name, so the things went into the right hands. He said his name was Stevens. He demanded my name and where I worked; I couldn't get out of there fast enough. I came back to the shop to warm you to tell Mr. Lumsden. You said later he went to Dundas. Mr. Stevens' son is the one who is giving me such trouble now. I must do his math homework, or he'll say I'm a labourer. When it isn't perfect, he says I'm making mistakes to make him look bad. That's usually when I get the soup poured down my back at lunch."

"They will move on," Richard sympathized.

He knew the same isolation. It was the same war he thought he'd left in Limerick.

"I think it would be a good idea for you to work

with a private teacher on the mathematics over the next year and in the day, come to work again with me at The Gazette. There are changes being talked about that might suit you well. If you came back, those ideas might become reality. They won't without someone like you. It's the same players in the shop. You know them all. They're good at what they do, but the world is changing beneath our feet. Before long, we'll be left trying to stand in midair."

"What are you talking about exactly?" John had lifted his eyes.

"In New York, newspapers are selling for a penny a copy – full broadsheets two-sided. They're not filled with the latest events in the legislature, but copy paid for by local merchants to promote their wares. Each merchant buys a piece of the page of each issue. They tell what they're selling or how special it is, or when it's arriving. When they pay for that space, it means the paper doesn't have to collect as much money from their subscribers and street sales. I want to try that out at The Gazette."

"What does Stanton think of that?" asked John Harvey.

"He doesn't! He's in a terrible state because Lord Sydenham died. Sydenham promised to make Stanton Queen's Printer for both the Canadas under the new Legislature, but Lord Stanley who is taking over, won't be honouring that commitment. Things are going to change, and I have been thinking about that a lot."

"Surely they'll have to have a Queen's Printer," said John Harvey.

"I can't see how they can do without it. The Government pumps out laws and changes and directives like windmills. They need secure and safe ways to prepare and distribute that work so that the information doesn't leak out to the advantage of the unscrupulous. We've shown we do that well. I hope it's enough to keep us in our jobs. But if that is all we do; the presses will sit idyll half the time. It is why we have a newspaper as well. The paper promotes the government view of the world. But there are other newspapers now that do that for them. I can see a day when promoting government policy will be in the hands of the entrepreneurs who benefit from those policies. When that happens, why would the government pay for what they get for free?"

John Harvey was looking at his father steadily, weighing the words.

"Look at what the Patriot is doing! Family Compact thought trumpeted to the last lead line. But the newspapers will have to make money other ways, and that is where merchants can pay the bills."

It was a dramatic vision of the future that he offered, and Richard ended it by saying, "You could start up the process of getting merchants to promote their products through our paper. It will be small to start, but I believe it is what we have to do. Would you like to come back and see if it's something that interests you?"

"Well it would beat going to school by a country mile!" John Harvey smiled.

*

"September 19, 1844."

Walter Rose, Richard's long-standing committee companion in the Masons, was holding up a copy of the Upper Canada Gazette and announcing the date to all within earshot.

"Congratulations, Watson on your first edition of The Gazette over your own name."

Those nearby at the bar in the Masonic Hall added their raised glasses and a chorus of, "Hear! Hear!"

As the rest of the companions settled back to their own conversations, Walter leaned forward and cut right to the heart of the takeover.

"What will be your editorial policy?"

"I've never known you to waste time in preliminaries," joked Richard. "Well, you'll just have to wait and see. But I'm not going to compete with Ryerson and the Christian Guardian or The Patriot at the other end. We can build on the successes that my son has accomplished with getting merchants to advertise in a penny paper. That has started well, and we are not close to meeting the demand we have. I think I'll be opening a new newspaper with a commercial and practical focus to take advantage of the immigrant trade."

"And you have little competition as well. Would that be in the back of your mind?" assessed Walter.

Richard just smiled.

"Got a name for it yet?" Walter persisted.

"The Canadian has the sound I like and is in tune with the times now the Upper and Lower provinces have been unified into one. What do you think?"

"It's what's under the masthead that will sell it – or not. I'll watch for it. Got someone who can run it?"

"I've got a man in mind that I apprenticed with in Limerick. He's been doing construction while he's learned all the reading and writing skills, he needs to manage a print shop. When we started out twenty-five years ago, he could fix anything that broke down. He's a good man; If I can get him, he'd make the plan work."

"Sounds like the paper will be on the street soon."

"Well we have to get through the wedding first," Richard drew a hand through his hair and shook his head. "If I live to be a hundred, I'll not see more confusion and fussing – and over what? Buttons and lace! Who and who not to invite seems to take an act of the Legislature. Teas up one arm and down the other. It was like pulling teeth to get them to agree on the wording of the invitations. Got them done anyway, and the Cathedral booked. If I just stay out of sight till the day, I think it sounds like a good idea," Richard groaned with just a hint of pride.

"Your daughter's name is …"

"Sarah!" Richard filled in quickly. "She's marrying Henry Price, the young lawyer, Harold and Helen Price's son. The two have known each other since they were children. It's a good match," concluded Richard.

"Well this will be the practice round eh? Don't you have a house full of daughters?"

"I certainly do," Richard sighed.

*

As they lay in bed staring up into the darkness, Maryanne sighed, "That was a lovely evening with the Prices."

She was reflecting on the invitation from her daughter, Sarah, to Sarah's own home earlier that evening. Sarah had invited Henry's parents - Harold and Helen – as well as themselves and had done herself proud – as usual.

Others had joined the party after dinner for the festivities.

"She's got enough silver flatware and serving dishes to set for twelve now," Maryanne added. "Henry's law practice must be doing well. And setting the table with all those tiny flags to celebrate the Queen's Birthday was so charming," she continued.

"It was a handsome roast of beef, I thought. What did she use to sweeten the rhubarb pie?" Richard felt obliged to keep up his end of the conversation, but he was fading fast.

"That was sugar from Jamaica, she told me!" Said Maryanne.

"Things must really be looking up if they can afford that!" Commented Richard. "Whose idea was the fireworks display?"

"Henry organized that."

"A bit over the top if you don't mind me saying." The comment got him a jab in the ribs.

"I didn't see Anna and John. I thought they were coming with Kivas and his wife?" He was referring to his daughter Anna Helena and the man with whom she was currently keeping company, John Tully. Protocol demanded that they be chaperoned when together, but Anna constantly challenged that practice, to her father's huge annoyance.

"They were there. I saw them for the drinks after the fireworks. I must have missed them when Kivas and Jane arrived," murmured Maryanne.

"I wish we could count on that child to do anything she says she'll do," Richard blurted out. "She's as angular as a picket fence about doing anything she's told. I've grown so embarrassed with her challenges to parental authority, I hate to use the name of her godparent especially in Helen's presence."

"Children are like that sometimes," Maryanne replied as she drifted to sleep.

Richard on the other hand was now fully awake, simmering over Anna Helena's catalogue of flaunting abuses. She questioned every expected behaviour of those with whom they now associated. Her behaviour insulted all with whom he had tried so hard to find acceptance.

*

Richard was scarlet with rage. One broken chair lay in his wake among the shards of his teacup along the far wall of the kitchen. He was stomping back and forth in the kitchen, crashing his feet on the pine board floor. On the next turn of the room he slammed the door hard enough to rattle the dishes in the cupboard.

"When did she tell you?"

"Yesterday, but I've suspected she was pregnant for some time," Maryanne said.

"Who's the father?"

"John, of course," Maryanne replied with a toss of her head.

"Why, of course? She's put herself in the place of any street-walker in town."

"It's John," whispered Maryanne

"Well she'd better get married right away. I'll stop by the church today."

The conversation was going as badly as Maryanne had expected.

"What a stupid, willful child! God Damn her!"

"Don't ever say that Richard," Maryanne shouted back as she slammed her hand on the table. "She is your daughter and she never deserves such scorn. You just remember when you were that age!'"

Richard stiffened at the rebuke. That took the wind out of his sails. Richard slumped to another chair.

"She isn't even eighteen yet!" He muttered with fading heat. "What kind of example is that to the others?"

"A cautionary one, I should think," Maryanne observed wryly with raised eyebrows.

The silence lengthened before Richard scraped back his chair, stood slowly and looked at the broken chair against the wall. He stepped to the wreckage, picked up a broken leg and rungs, stomped on the back to complete the destruction, and threw the pieces into the kindling box.

*

It was later in the week when Richard and Maryanne were again in the kitchen after supper. He had arranged for a wedding ceremony two weeks hence at St. James Cathedral. Maryanne told Anna about the arrangements and said that she could let out a dress for Anna so that her condition would not be obvious. The conversation with Anna had not gone well. Before she conveyed the results to Richard, she made sure to clear the table completely.

"Anna said she'd think about it."

"Think about what?"

"The wedding date you arranged at the cathedral."

With shock growing into teeth-clenched anger, Richard slowly folded the newspaper he had been reading and refolded it and creased it strongly into a baton and put his hands on the arms of his chair.

"What do you mean, she's *thinking* about it?"

"She hasn't decided she wants to marry just then."

Richard's colour was rising to red in the lamplight, "Well she has to get married by then to avoid a scandal. How long does she think people can be deceived? Not everyone does arithmetic as slowly as she does. Of course, she'll be married as we arranged!"

"Richard," Maryanne said with earnest intent as she laid a hand on his forearm, "I think you better get used to the idea that she'll marry when she decides, and if it is going to be a scandal, it might be the whole purpose of this pregnancy."

Richard's face was blood red now. Maryanne had never seen him so angry. But Richard sat and twisted the newspaper in his hands to shreds. Abruptly, he shot to his feet tipping over his chair, hurled the newspaper onto the table and slammed out of the back door loudly enough to rattle the dishes again.

The soldiers from the garrison brought him home dead drunk late that night and just laid him on the kitchen floor to wake up. Maryanne, alone in bed upstairs, heard them come in and gently close the door on leaving. She did not come down.

*

It was just before Christmas. Maryanne and Anna Helena were talking at the kitchen table by lamplight, when Richard came in late and unsteadily. He squinted at the women while he leaned on the doorpost for support before staggering to his chair at the end of the table and falling into it.

Maryanne immediately rose and poured a tepid cup of tea from the teapot into a metal mug and handed it to Richard. He downed a gulp with a groan and sat back bleary-eyed.

"John and I have arranged to be married on January thirty first," Anna Helena announced.

Richard swatted the words away with a backhand wave as he slumped forward.

"You'll not be invited unless you pledge to arrive sober," Anna continued. "In your present condition, you're a disgrace!"

"*I'm* a disgrace," slurred Richard, "Hah!"

"Every accusation you've thrown at me, every scandal you've laid at my door can just as easily be found at yours, Father. You are the disgrace we all make excuses for. The sympathy my friends and acquaintances express to me in the market and on the street, is not because of my so-called condition, but because I have a father that is dead drunk nightly in the pub. Does he beat you? They ask, he couldn't and wouldn't dare, is what I tell them!" She spat the words out in a spray, "You talk about example to your other children. Look at the example you hold up to them. Where I show them love, what do you display? Even your son has gone elsewhere to work so badly, have his efforts been acknowledged,"

Anna shouted. The accusations hung in the air.

Richard finished his tea, stood slowly and walked upstairs to bed.

"The doctor tells me the baby," Anna said with competitive pride, "Isn't due till the end of February," Anna said to Maryanne after Richard had left.

Anna relished that her child would be the first grandchild. Sarah wasn't even pregnant yet.

Maryanne looked up from her hands folded on the table before her and asked quietly, "Who's the doctor?"

"Burnside. He's a friend of John's"

"Is he caring for you well?"

"Yes mother. I'll be fine," Anna said as she laid a hand on Maryanne's. "I'll be fine."

What do you know? Thought Maryanne. The memory of a dead child in her lap in the hold of a sailing ship tossing over the waves rose up unbidden. She couldn't say anything though, because of her tears. She simply clutched Anna's hand so hard it hurt.

*

Richard and Maryanne were talking across the gulf that seemed to separate them in their bed the night of the

Christening. Richard was stone-cold sober and had been since the Christmas confrontation with his daughter.

They had stood at the back of the church where they could deny involvement, while the Christening of their first grandchild was going on at the front. Richard had noticed that Kivas and his wife were not in the circle around the font. Richard had asked John Harvey if he

would stand with his sister as the family representative and John had agreed because Anna had already asked him. Richard was grateful for that.

"I noticed neither of our family names was given to the child, Tully's nor ours," Richard was trying to hide his pain behind nonchalance.

"Yes," Maryanne agreed in a whisper. Then she added after a moment of silence, "She almost lost it, Richard."

"Lost what?"

"The baby!"

Richard was stunned. What bitterness kept that from him? "I hadn't heard."

"The baby came early and was backwards. Without Doctor Burnside's help, the baby and Anna both might have died. It's why she named him 'Alexander Burnside'. But she did make his first name 'John'. It is a name from your family." Maryanne was trying to pull ends together.

"And the bugger who got her that way. I doubt she had any intention of honouring her Watson heritage when she named her child. Another finger in our eye is what it was!"

"You don't know that, Richard," Maryanne

cautioned.

"And likely never will," Richard replied as he turned towards the cold edge of his bed.

18
THE CANADIAN

Richard had another pair of newly arrived Irishmen in tow when he arrived at Harold Price's new building site. Price was deep in conversation with George Crawford, his foreman as they approached. Richard and Co. stood quietly waiting for the others to finish. Harold at last turned and was surprised.

"Sorry, I didn't know you were standing there. Have you got more workers for me?"

Price was already appraising the ragged men beside Richard.

"Yes. This is James Bennis. His Da' was a blacksmith on our street when I lived in Limerick, and this is his friend Thomas Brady. They both are newly arrived and need to get started at something. Could they work for you for a couple weeks to get their feet under them? They want to bring families later. I explained the arrangement you made with Sean and the test you set. I think they will serve you well, but these men are special, and it is about their skills I want to talk you, Harold"

Harold appraised the new men as did George. Harold nodded and George drew them aside to explain their duties, and how they would be paid.

When the men were far enough away, Richard continued, "Bennis learned blacksmithing in his father's shop, but they were starving there no matter what they did. He's brought some tools, but he needs a place to work. He's tried the shops around, but they only want apprentices. There isn't enough room for two smiths to work in most shops. I wanted to ask on his behalf, if you could finance an anvil, brick for him to build a forge and starting stock. That's not all. He needs a place to build his shop. I know you have lot on King Street. Maybe a blacksmith shop would be a good use for it."

"That lot is too big for just his shop," observed Price.

"That's where Brady comes in. He's a cooper by trade. I was thinking that if he set up next door, or behind the blacksmith shop, and you encouraged Bennis to make only the hoops for barrels till he got established, it would cut down on the cost for starting stock, and give both jobs. If you could get the chimney heat from the forge to heat the water to bend the barrel staves, that might be to the benefit of both. I could look out for a carpenter or carriage maker among the immigrants to build wagons in the rest of the lot."

"Why don't they get a loan at the bank?" Harold asked.

"They're Irish, Harold," Richard exclaimed as

though he had to state the obvious. "There is no way they can get credit at any bank around here. You know how the bankers look them. They don't have a chance. But if you wanted to get your finger into another pie, this could be a profitable venture for all concerned."

"That's an interesting idea, Watson. Let me think on it till the weekend. We'll see how they work here." Then after a pause Harold asked, "You intrigue me with this thought about using the heat that leaves the forge to heat water for the cooper. How did you come up with that?"

"Blame my wife. She has a large kettle sitting on the back of the stove all the time. I kid her that it is to make tea, but she has a smaller kettle for that. She loads the small one from the larger and the water is already warm. It just seemed like another way to use the same idea."

"Glad you're a printer," quipped Harold. "I wouldn't want you for a competitor." He slapped Richard on the back, "See you on the weekend."

*

Richard's start-up newspaper The Canadian was consuming his time in ways he had not planned. As long as John Harvey had been selling advertising, he'd been able to keep his attention on The Gazette. After all, The Gazette was what was paying the bills, and some for The Canadian as well. But it was obvious that he was running out of hours in the day. Sean O'Connor had become his foreman and right-hand man in the shop after he had learned to read and write. In that he was invaluable. But Sean had little business sense. His strengths were his intuitive mechanical talent, a gift of the gab and a magnet for all things Irish.

Because of the huge numbers of Irish immigrants that were arriving every year because of the Famine, the local rooming houses had stopped advertising in his paper. Rooms were snapped up by first comers leaving the homeowners fighting off desperate requests for accommodation continually. The Canadian office had become a clearinghouse for accommodation in private homes. Essentially, Richard was pre-selecting boarders and sending only enough to fill the rooms that the owner said were available. The owners were glad not to have fights on the porch and paid to prove it. Sean seemed to know every Irish family in town and was constantly asking them to take new arrivals, even for only a few days, till they could move on to farms, of railway jobs in Hamilton. It had almost ended the gouging practices along the waterfront where the gullible and exhausted had been preyed upon.

Maryanne was regularly asking the farmers in the market for places where immigrants could find work and a place to live. She brought that information to Richard over dinner. It was she who suggested a new focus for The Canadian for the winter months.

"Should the paper be offering help to those learning to read and write?" She asked. "If there was space in a corner to place a single letter of the alphabet in capital and lower-case letters, printed and in script, people who don't write now might have a reason to collect the papers and practice during the winter. In another corner, you might add stories for others to read. You mentioned how well received the work of Charles Dickens was received when it was printed in serial fashion in London. Could we do likewise?"

"Are there things that women need to know about how to get through the winter that they don't know when they get off the ship?" Asked Richard.

"Of course!" Answered Maryanne with a wave of her hand to indicate the huge size of the topic. "At the top of the list is how to keep warm personally and keep food. Our Irish kin never had to deal with a Canadian winter. Potatoes and cabbages can't freeze. Meat and fruit can. And then there are the different sources of food and what to do with each.

"I think I'd add how to make clothes over, so they are warmer in the winter," offered Mary from her corner of the room where she was doing her writing exercises, "and how to make mittens."

"We could make a list of things that people have to trade, not for money, but for labour. We'd charge the person with those things a small amount to advertise them in the paper. We could make a list of where to get things, from apples to wool. Perhaps the churches could buy a few spinning wheels or looms and offer them free or at a nominal rent, to women to spin wool on their own and even make cloth if they have that skill. Do you think there would be much resentment from the local merchants or spinners and weavers?"

Everyone was getting rather excited as the ideas bounced around the room from one to the other. A silence filled the space after so much talking and into it, Richard tossed a final thought.

"Maryanne," Richard asked, "do you think that you, Mary and Sophia could write up such material every week so it could become a regular feature of the newspaper?"

"How many cold meals can you eat? Could you learn to wear dirty clothes?"

That brought the conversation to a silent stop that night, but Richard could see the topic would come up again.

*

Richard was entering the receipts from his engraving and calling cards into his ledger at The Gazette office. It was past closing; all the workmen had left, when a tap came at the door. Through the window beside the door he could see two ragged men waiting outside.

"Can't help you tonight," he called through the door. "We open at eight o'clock."

He could not make out the muffled reply, but it was immediately followed by another tapping at the door. He picked up the stove poker and strode to the door. Placing his foot behind the door, he unlocked it and opened it a crack.

"Sorry, I can do nothing for you tonight, gentlemen. Come and see me tomorrow," he said to the shapes.

"Mr. Watson," said one. "We did not come for help. You have helped us beyond measure already. It's Bennis, sir and Brady. We came to thank you for talking to Mr. Price and tell you what he's offered."

Richard opened the door a few inches more and could see the faces of the two men he'd taken to work at Price's building project two weeks before.

"Yes, men. How has it worked out?" Richard asked. He wasn't about to let them into the office at this late hour. Though he opened the door more, he still yet kept his foot behind it and the poker concealed.

"Mr. Price is going to build us a combined blacksmith and cooperage on a lot down the street," Brady said. "He'll build accommodation over it as a boarding house for now, but assures us that our families can take over the space when they arrive next year."

"I get to build the forge," Bennis interrupted. "But Mr. Price wants to have some sort of water heating thing built into the chimney. I told him he can't do that without affecting the draft on the fire. But I think we can work out a damper that will give me full draft when I need it. He says he'll supply the metal from America and an anvil for me and provide oak for Brady from the lumberyard for a share in our businesses. We'll have a lease on the building for ten years and then we can negotiate changes. Nobody could ask for more Sir. We came to say thank you for your help." Both men extended their hands slowly.

Richard shook each in turn, but he still held the door as it was with his foot.

"Well good luck then. When will you be starting to build?"

"We dig the foundation for the forge tomorrow. The building will go up around us as we work. We could be pounding iron in two weeks, but I fear it will take longer than that to get metal from America. But Brady can start shaping staves for his barrels. I'll be busy building a workbench and storage racks."

It was plain the men couldn't wait to get started.

Richard raised his eyebrows as he asked, "When you are digging the foundation for the forge, I'd suggest you dig down at least three feet, maybe four. I know it will take more bricks or stone to come back up to floor level, but the winter frost won't heave it later. Spread the dirt you remove around the floor to raise it above street level. You'll see why when the streets are flooded next spring. Check with Crawford. He'll be able to advise you. Oh yes - from one husband to another. Your wives will thank you forever if, while you're digging, you dig a hole about six feet deep, six wide and long. Cover it with a solid covering and a trap door so you can get into it. Shore it up so it won't collapse in. When your families come, they'll be wanting that space to store food for the winter. It keeps cold all year but won't freeze. Put some shelves or platforms to keep things up off the ground, and you'll be the envy of every neighbour on the street."

"Never heard of that," said Bennis suspiciously.

"Have I steered you wrong yet?" asked Richard.

The men shook their heads.

"Believe me then," said Richard. "Check with Crawford on it also. He can probably find some scrap that will do well for shoring up the walls. Don't let him raise your lease rate because of it because you say you are improving his property at no cost to him. Tell him Watson told you so. He'll agree. Oh, one thing more! Do you think that we could hold a supper for the Irish community in your shop when you open? You just provide the space. Everyone who comes brings food to share. Talk to Graham at his tavern about a keg of ale. He's good at keeping control of things and you don't have to worry about someone else's liquor. It's a Canadian tradition you'll find."

Both men looked a bit puzzled by yet another suggestion.

"Can we talk to you about that later," they asked.

"I'll stop by someday this week and we can talk then," Richard smiled, "Goodnight! And again, good luck to you both."

Richard closed the door and latched it and sat down as

the men walked away. *That was a good day's work,* he thought.

*

Another ship had dumped six hundred more Irish immigrants on the waterfront of Toronto harbour! Maryanne had lost track of the total number that had come to the offices of The Canadian for help. There had been thousands so far this year, she was sure. She and the girls had joined Richard for half-time on the days after ships docked and the whole family was as exhausted as the gaunt refugees that were guided to their door. Sean, their foreman at the newspaper, and his helpers had distributed handouts to those who had been cleared by the staff at the Fever Sheds.

"Here, take this," he'd say as he handed a poster to a family stepping out on the street looking around in confusion. "He has a kitchen set up. You'll have stew in your hands in 10 minutes – for all of you. You'll find the latest list of places to stay where you really can sleep safely tonight. He has the latest list of jobs and it won't cost you a penny. He's one of us." As often as not, the adult who received the poster simply looked back, further frustrated because they couldn't read.

"Take it to The Canadian Office down the street there. Sean was pointing and had a hand on the man's shoulder gently steering him in the right direction. You won't miss it. Past the Blacksmith and the Wagon builder. Bennis is the smith's name. He comes from Limerick. Where are you from?"

Sean made sure he had big and burly company when he interrupted any gougers who hadn't gotten the message and were still trying to bilk money from such people for accommodation or food that didn't exist. Sean would just push past the thief and thrust a poster into the hand of his countryman and start talking. When Sean's confederate came up close behind the scoundrel it usually stopped any further attempt to coerce the immigrants.

Maryanne had felt she had won the world the day she had convinced the administrators at the hospital to offer immigrant women employment for a few days to wash sheets if the hospital would cover the cost of bleach, soap, barrels and washboards. Richard had browbeaten the councilors of the city to link washing services and grave digging to meals, accommodation in canvas tents and a pittance of a wage. But at least it was a start. There were many who resented the Irish presence in the city, and of course there were a few rowdies, and barroom brawls to justify the arrogance. It only took a few to tar all with that brush.

Richard found that The Canadian, changed its focus as soon as the Immigrant ships stopped for the season. As long as immigrants were arriving, they wanted to know where jobs were. The Great Western Railway was laying track so they could use many labourers. Some could obtain farms if they wanted to travel far enough. Many sought to labour in cities with various tradesmen. Matching labour to those needing it was an exhausting process, but it is what the Watson's were devoted to when the need arose. Because of his connections with the other newspapers and now telegraph, Richard was better than most. But when the boats stopped, Richard was implementing the reading and writing ideas Maryanne had suggested.

In the winter his newspaper carried the news people would pay to find out about. Richard chose his vocabulary to encourage the new news readers. Sean had regular contributions that emphasized the Irish neighbourhood. Maryanne had even taken to offering an advice section for coping with winter. After all, Sophia Dalton had taken over The Patriot when her husband died and was running it successfully. Why shouldn't there be a place for women in the newspaper business! But winter was ending, and the days were getting longer, the streets soggier.

*

It was dark and cold in the bedroom and again both lay snuggled tightly together under their quilts.

"It will be our second grandchild," Maryanne whispered.

They hadn't talked about Anna Helena's second pregnancy since she told Richard two days ago. Instead of storming out, as she had half suspected, Richard had just groaned and held his head in his hands.

"I hope it will go well," sighed Richard, "but I can talk to a total stranger from three thousand miles away more easily than I can talk to Anna. I fear there is no healing that hurt now. It is a regret I carry."

"Do you suppose we might imagine a reconciliation?" The silence deepened and thickened.

"That is a lot to ask, Maryanne."

"Do you suppose we could meet for tea. That's not long and it could be a start. Easter is coming. Maybe they could come for tea after church, in the spirit of the day?"

There was another long pause during which Maryanne held her breath. She wondered if Richard would answer at all.

"I'll try, Maryanne, Richard sighed. "Lord knows I wish we could be at ease with each other. It's not fair to the little ones to load them with the bitterness of their elders. You'll arrange it then? For April eighth?"

But he could feel his gut tighten, his mind started to race.

"Thank you, Richard. I'll talk to her."

Amens were said with the same reverence. Richard was struggling to lift his gloom. He was trying to picture boosting his grandson onto his knee. He suddenly imagined carving toys for him as he had done for his own children. His pen knife went still into his pocket before all else in the morning and was wearing holes with the same regularity. He wondered if he should start to-morrow. Have a gift to offer as a token peace offering? Easter was a couple weeks off. There was time. He had decided to do so when Maryanne interrupted his thoughts.

"You won't go drinking again, will you?" Maryanne was beseeching him remembering the last time, "You frighten me when you do."

"I'll go for a drink with the men, but they won't have to carry me home."

19

THE FIRE

It was the night of Good Friday. The Christians were preparing to celebrate their holiest of days. The lapsed were just celebrating – as though they needed a reason. Richard had been asked to join the Militia to tour the downtown area during the evening.

Someone had asked if they were a Peacekeeping Force but the attempt at a joke had fallen flat. There were too many Irish within earshot and too many bad hometown memories came with the term. But in the interest of Peace, Order, and Good Government, it was felt that if uniformed men were seen in numbers in the area of any revelry, it kept the brawls to a minimum.

Richard wasn't really a member of the Militia, but he was asked to join in the group because of his association with so many of the recent Irish immigrants. He knew many in the community and was known by more because for the help he had organized for them. When you can call a man by his name, it helps to keep control, so Richard was asked to join the others for the night.

Teams of Militia, in uniform, had wandered the Market Block since sunset, chatting to all and showing the flag, as it was called. They had all decided to meet back at Graham's Tavern at the end of the evening and so it was, at midnight, that they were gathered for a good-night drink. Richard found himself elbow to elbow at the end of the well-worn table with Sergeant Robert Crockett. Both were half-way down the mug of ale that sat in a wet ring before them.

"Going to the Sunrise Service?" Crockett asked of Richard.

Richard caught himself before he rudely evaluated that idea, smiled, and replied simply. "No! You?"

"Likewise." Crockett paused before he added, "But you know if I was, I'd just keep drinking here till then so I could go straight from here."

"I think you'd not be welcome in that condition," cautioned Richard

"Likely right." Crockett took another sip from his mug

"The wife has a tea planned with my daughter and her family. I'd better be there and on my best behaviour,"

Richard said.

"Is that the one who married the lawyer?" asked Crockett

"No. The other one – Anna Helena," Richard replied. It had been a long time since he had used her full name. "She married John Tully, the architect. She's expecting a new baby in the Fall. I thought I'd get started making a collection of animal toys for the child. I did the same for my own children."

Richard pulled the completed palm-sized figure from his pocket along with his pen knife. Crockett had known about Richard's whittling skills for a long time. He picked up the piece and admired it in the lamplight. Richard had pulled his knife from his pocket. When Richard took back the carving, he scraped smooth a rough spot that he'd spotted in the oblique light. He set his knife beside his mug.

"All the horses I know stand on four legs. You have them standing on a platform," the sergeant observed.

"It makes the carving more durable. If you have legs sticking out, they regularly get broken off. When they are all joined by this platform, they don't break so easily," Richard explained. "It looks like it is standing in a pasture and it gives the child something to chew on without worrying about him swallowing anything. You know how a baby chews a lot."

Crockett nodded knowingly and then continued, "Nice knife."

Richard held it up and flicked the pin that secured the blade in and out, in the light of the lamp then handed it to Crockett to admire – and return. The story of the blade with its locking pin that came from so long ago quickly followed. Next to his story about the first battle fought by the Cameronians at Dunkeld, it was the story for which he was best known.

"Enough!" Richard drained his mug, stood and pocketed toy and pen knife.

He noticed the smell of smoke when he stood and at the same time someone shouted, *Fire!* The back door of the tavern to the privy had been swung open by another drinker heading to relieve himself. Through the open door, Richard caught the reflection of a substantial blaze. The door itself was alight.

"Did the privy explode?" Joked someone. They couldn't see what Richard could. "I told Graham not to put a lamp out there!" The old joke was followed by a chorus of loud laughs. "Who had beans for dinner?"

More hoots and table thumping followed that addition. The haw-hawing quickly died as those closest renewed the call.

"Fire! Fire!" more voices shouted. "Get water! Quickly!"

From his place, Richard could see through the door that a pile of waste lumber and shingles under the eaves was already aflame, head high. A part bucket of water from the bar hit the flames on the door that hung inward and quenched them. The scorched door stood black and smoking but the fire outside, was raging now.

"Break up that fire," someone shouted.

"Bring a bench to push it away."

There was a stumbling of bodies as those who grasped the urgency turned back into the pub and were blocked by those gawking at the flames.

"Get out of the way, you fool!"

Pushing and shoving bodies jammed the doorway. Two men managed to grab both ends of a bench and rush through the door. They trod on the shards of a broken lamp as they set the bench down. The men moved side by side with the bench between them so they could they could swing it like a battering ram trying to knock the blazing boards away from the house. All they did was spread the fire along the wall. They hooked the leg over some boards and pulled them free but now the wall was ablaze, and the cedar shingles of the overhanging roof suddenly flickered and flared up.

Others now joined the first two with new benches but already the fire had crept up the roof beyond reach. One militiaman was flailing the fire on the ground with his coat. Everyone was in each other's way. Someone else arrived with a bucket of water from the horse trough down the street. The water arched up onto the roof but missed the center of the burning shingles. The fire had now crept along the wall and was poking fingers up through the eave further down. Crockett recognized what that meant.

"If it gets into the roof, it's gone lads. Get anything you can to knock down those shingles."

Quickly each effort proved the benches were too short, the wall was burning too hotly to get closer, and there was not enough water. The Sergeant grasped the change before the others. He started shouting to those still inside.

"Run for the Fire Brigade; organize a bucket brigade from the horse trough. Run Men! Run!"

Richard dashed into the street. Already sparks were leaping into the air. The fire was at the ridge of the roof moving along fresh shingles like a living thing. Four buckets had appeared. It was not enough. The street suddenly was alive with people, shouting, bumping into each other, arms full of things. Richard turned to see through the open front door of the pub, that the inside was now burning fiercely. He bumped into someone carrying bolts of cloth from a store next to the pub, into the street. It had happened so fast.

Flames were shooting, bursting through the front of the Tavern roof. There was no way to stop this fire now. Richard ran for the office of the Patriot newspaper office a few doors along the street. He knew the office well. He had been friends, if competitors, with the owners for years. He had to save the type. With type, the newspaper could limp past this disaster. Without it, the Patriot could be finished.

Richard pounded and pounded on the front door shouting the warning. He pounded more. The young apprentice stumbled to the door trying to shake the sleep away. His mouth fell open as he saw the street awash in orange light. He recognized Richard from his being in the shop to visit the owners many times, but it was the awful light in the tree that he couldn't stop looking at.

"Come with me now," Richard ordered.

"I don't have me boots," the kid complained.

"Get 'em fast and come upstairs."

Richard had already turned and was headed for the outside staircase to the type setting room above the print shop. Richard smashed open the door with a well-placed kick. The flaring light from the street danced menacingly through the windows that normally let in sunlight.

He could see about a dozen trays of type set on the workbenches all around the room and as many more stacked in the cupboard. He strode across the room and grabbed a tray. He squinted at the type it contained, and the tray beside. A double stack was too heavy for him to lift with his weak arm. He hefted them one at a time to the door. The apprentice had just arrived.

"Take these across the street. Put them behind the rain barrel there and come back for more."

"I can't carry them both. They're too heavy."

"One at a time then! Hurry! Don't dump them." The lad struggled down the steps with the weighty tray of lead type. Richard headed back into the building. He had two more trays out on the landing where the smoke didn't burn his eyes before he realized they were the font for calling cards. He set them down on the landing of the stairs and ran back into the room.

This time he crossed the room to the cupboard where the Capital Letters and larger type sizes were stored. He jerked out one tray after another until he found the type font for the newspaper he had given to the apprentice first. There were two more trays, no three. Wait, these trays were mixed up. He pulled more trays from the cupboard to find matching material. He stacked correct trays in pairs and hauled them to the doorway. These weren't as heavy because the letters were large and fewer. The lad was just returning up the stairs.

"Take these also."

He set them down on the landing and fled back inside the room. Smoke filled the room now. But Richard was slowly gathering up the different sizes of the type fonts in their trays and handing them to the apprentice who was running as fast as he could. Unless he could get all the trays of each font, those he had saved would be of no use. You couldn't run out of one font and use a different one to finish printing a job.

"These go with the first ones you took out. Go quickly. There are three more."

The room was stifling now. Richard knew the downstairs must be on fire. He knew if the solvents they used for cleaning type ever caught fire, the place would explode. Richard stacked two more trays on each other and scrambled for the door. The fire was roaring now. He could hardly shout over it.

"There's one more," he shouted to the apprentice.

His words were swept away by the crash of flames bursting through the back window of the shop downstairs.

"It's time to go," screamed the lad as he took one of the trays from Richard.

"Time enough yet," Richard wheezed and spun on his heel.

The apprentice had stacked his rescued type with the rest and turned back when the floor of the upper room collapsed into the inferno that had been the print shop. The child dropped like a brick beside the piles of type and wept. Across the street was a tower of flame, sparks streaking into the sky. The fire was pulsing like thunder. It was a hypnotic sight. As the heat punched through his coat, it jarred the lad into action. He pulled a sleeve across his face and crouched behind the rain barrel.

Then on second thought he jumped into the barrel and pulled the cover over top of his head. The barrel was half full and cool on his skin. He cowered in the smelly space shaking with fear as the fire raged down the other side of the street swallowing one building after another.

*

The voices were far away when the apprentice poked his sooty face out of the rain barrel that had saved his life. What was left of the buildings across the street was still burning hotly but the walls of flame were gone. Only quiet crackling from spent fires was close at hand. He clambered out and stood there, soaking wet beside the type he had helped to save. The rising sun was slanting through the gloom. Where else could he go? He was supposed to be in the shop and have the stove going. That was his job. But there was no shop now. So, he just slumped there beside his type trays amid the smoke and ashes with his nose tucked under his wet sleeve to keep the smoke out of his face. That's where he was when Edward O'Brien and Mrs. Dalton found him. Mrs. Dalton had been the owner of The Patriot until last Fall, when O'Brien took over, but it was a transfer in name only. Mrs. Dalton showed up all the time - to advise, he was told. When Mrs. Dalton saw him, she hardly recognized the lad.

"Peter? Is it you?" She gripped his shoulder and turned his faced upwards.

"Yes ma'am," he coughed.

"How did you get out? And what is this?" she asked pointing at the trays of type.

"Mr. Watson woke me up when the fire started up the street. He brought these out to the top of the stairs and told me to put them here for safety."

"Where is Richard now?" She asked.

Peter simply nodded to the burning rubble where the shop had been.

"Oh no! No! That can't be. Surely!"

"He went back for one more tray, Ma'am. I told him it was time to get out, but he went back for the last one. When I got down here, I put what he gave me here," he looked down, "They were too heavy for me to carry two at a time. I was going back for another that he'd left on the stairs. When I turned around the whole building fell in. I didn't see him come out, but he might have while my back was turned. He was awfully tired. I suppose he could have escaped and be somewhere resting."

Peter became aware of another man standing nearby obviously listening in to the conversation. He was scribbling in a notepad. When the three turned to him, he tipped his soot-smeared hat bowed slightly to Mrs. Dalton.

"James Smith, reporter for The Globe," he said,

"Did I hear rightly. Richard Watson died?"

"We don't know that for sure," cautioned Mrs. Dalton, "Don't be spreading rumours."

"Maybe we could get the Fire Brigade from the Fireman's Hall up the way, to come and cool down the ashes to see if it's true," said O'Brien. "Peter, go see if you can find them and ask their chief to bring his men and equipment here. Tell him Mrs. Dalton asked and that we're looking for Mr. Watson. He'll know who it is."

*

The Fire Brigade was pumping water onto hot ashes and a few soldiers were poking through the rubble and scraps of partly burned beams with pikes and shovels wherever it was cool enough to stand. Word had spread as quickly as the fire, of a possible fatality. A few of the Militiamen with whom Richard had been drinking the night before had just joined the searchers. Robert Crockett was leading them in support of the soldiers from the garrison.

The bent wreckage of the press supported a tent of debris in a field of partly burned boards. When the first soldier hooked back one of the timbers propped on the metal and discovered a burnt boot, his whispered *Here he is*, seemed terribly loud among the muted scraping of the others nearby. Quickly the rest of the burned material over the body was pushed aside.

"God. There's hardly anything left of him,"

Crockett was immediately beside the first finder, "Get a blanket Private," Crockett ordered.

While everyone stepped back to let the Private do as he was ordered, Crockett knelt; There was a skull and some bones. Most of the flesh had been charred beyond recognition. He flipped off another small piece of wood covering the waist area of the corpse. Scraps of trousers had survived there. In the wrinkles of partly burned cloth was a lump of scorched wood in the shape of a horse, and a pen knife with a burnt wooden handle. When he lifted the remnants, he found that the blade still opened, and a metal pin held it in the open position when you pushed a lever with your finger.

"This is Mr. Watson," Crockett said quietly.

He raised his eyes to two other militiamen who looked on. The blanket was coming from the street.

"Go get a coffin, boys. Next street over." He tossed his head to indicate the direction. The sergeant carefully spread the blanket over the burnt body.

*

Everyone had retreated to the edge of the collapsed building when Maryanne ran up disheveled and soot stained. She recognized Robert right away.

"Have you seen Richard? He didn't come home last night. The men told me he was down here. They thought he might be resting around here." Words were pouring out of her in a hysterical stream.

"We found him Mrs. Watson. He's over there."

Crockett flicked his eyes towards the blanket covered heap. Maryanne followed his look then swung her eyes back to him.

"NO! Please no! That can't be him. Surely, he's around somewhere else. He's not at the office. I was just there. He has to be somewhere else."

Crockett opened his hand. In it was the burnt pen knife and the scorched wooden figure. Mary looked at the pieces, and back to Crockett's eyes and collapsed into a pile of skirts and the most heart-broken wailing he'd ever heard. The reporter ran off as all others bowed their heads in sorrow.

Duty's Dad

APPENDIX

BRITISH MONEY SYSTEM RICHARD USED

1 pound (£) equals 20 shillings (s) 1-shilling equals 12 pence (p) a crown is 5 shillings (1/4 of a pound) so half a crown is 2 shillings and 6 pence a guinea is 1 pound 1 shilling

*

There were different kinds of printing presses that Richard Watson might have been working on in the 1820's - 40's. This is a Harrild Press. Robert Harrild was born in 1790 in England. He worked in the book printing business early on, and then switched to manufacturing presses by 1832. His invention of rollers to ink the press was considered revolutionary at the time. After 1805 something like this might have been in the Print Shop.

Presses like these were operating in the 1820's

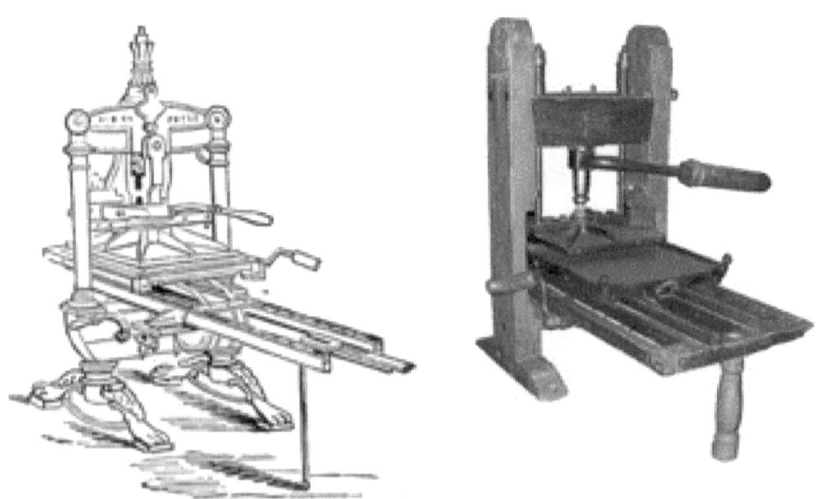

L) Lord Stanhope's Printing Press about 1848

R) Ramage Foolscap printer about 1820

These all show examples of presses where the letters
were fixed into a flat frame and the paper was pressed
down upon the inky letters to be printed. During this
same period, some manufacturers began to experiment
with rotary cylinders that held the type. Steam power
really made that style of press fly so that by the mid
1850's, only rotary cylinder presses were in regular use.
Older machines might survive in specialty shops or
backwaters.

A date of 1826 accompanies this press.

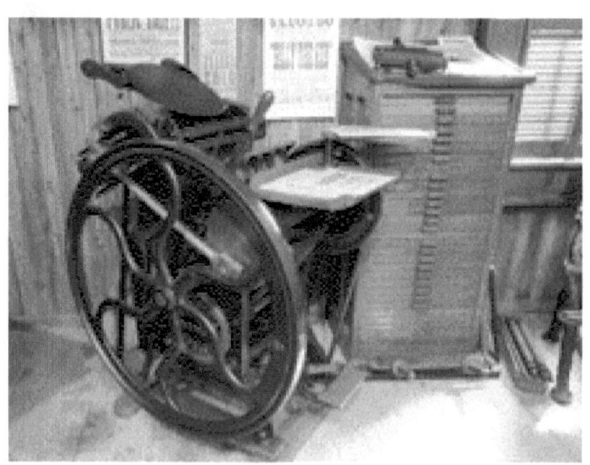

Printing press about 1805 by Granger

Note the storage cabinets for different type fonts. It is these trays that would have been spread all over the work benches at **The Patriot** on the night Richard was trying to find matching sets in the dark while the raging fire advanced on the building where he was working. Each tray would have looked like the one below. When filled with lead type, the tray could weigh 20-30 pounds. In the photograph on the left, the drawer handles on bottom trays are missing – maybe jerked off because the tray was so heavy.

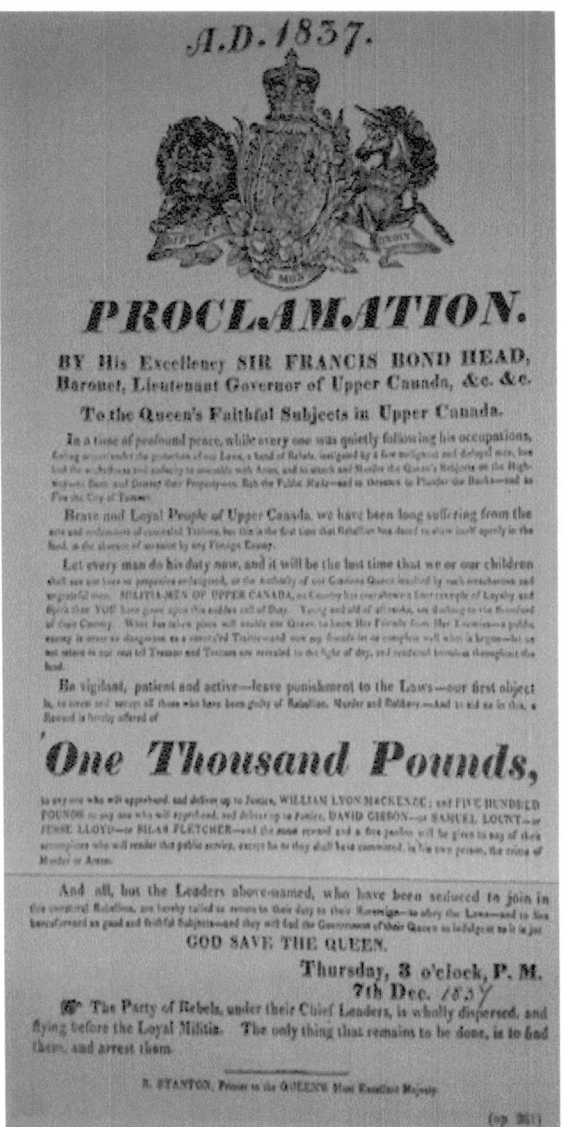

This document relates to Richard Watson, father of John Harvey Watson (Sr.). Richard was born in 1792 in Limerick, Ireland. He died on April 7, 1849, age 57, and was buried on April 9, 1849 in St James Cathedral Cemetery in Toronto.

The following is a verbatim transcript of a newspaper article which appears in **The Globe** newspaper on Wednesday April 11, 1849. **The Globe** only published on Wednesdays at the time. The article is transcribed because the projection of the microfilm was barely readable and the photocopy from the microfilm was even less so. The article refers to a fire in the business district on the morning of Saturday April 7, 1849. This copy was retyped from the copy made for the Watson Genealogy distributed in 2006 because I could not find the original file of that document.

Tremendous Fire!

Globe Office   Saturday Morning, 6 o'clock

About half past one this morning, a fire was discovered in some out houses in the rear of Graham's Tavern, King Street and Post's Tavern, Nelson Street. The fire speedily extended to the Main part of Nelson Street on the East, consuming Post's Tavern, the **Patriot** office &c. and turning into King Street to the East where it burnt all to Mr. Sproule's building where it stopped. The fire extended to the south of Duke Street, consuming nearly all the back buildings and the office of the Saving's Bank.

It then crossed to the west side of Nelson Street to Rolf's Tavern, destroying the whole block, including the *Mirror* office to Mr. Nasmith's bakery. Proceeding from Rolf's Tavern, the flames laid hold of the corner building occupied by Mr. O'Donohue, which was speedily consumed and then they ran along the whole block to Mr. O'Neill's consuming the valuable stores of Messrs. Hayes, Harris, Cheney, O'Neill and others. About three o'clock, the spire of St. James Cathedral took fire and the building was entirely destroyed. About the same time the flames broke out in the Old City Hall, consuming the greater part of the front buildings, including Mr. McFarlane's store.

The fire extended from the Cathedral across to the south side of King Street where a fire lately occurred. The shop of Mr. Rogers and others were, with difficulty, saved. Al the block extending to Mr. Walter McFarlane's store was in great danger, some of them had most of their goods removed and great injury to property was sustained. About 5 o'clock the flames were in great measure subdued. The exertions of the firemen were for a long time as usual, retarded by want of water. The soldiers of the Rifle Brigade from the garrison were extremely active and deserve the highest gratitude of the citizens. The loss is estimated at L 100,000 but this must be within the mark. We are happy to say that no life has been lost, although there were many narrow escapes.

FURTHER PARTICULARS

The above appeared in the greater part of last Saturday's impression. It is not easy to describe the gloom which this calamity has cast over the city, or the ruinous appearance of the ground so lately occupied by the many respectable and industrious individuals who, by the work of four or five hours were suddenly thrown out of business or seriously injured in their circumstances. The losses from this calamity will be best ascertained from the following statement, copied in part from yesterday's *Colonist* and derived from other sources of information.

Church of England Cathedral insured for L 8,500, cost of building from L 11,000 to L 13,000. O'Neill Brothers building insured for L 1,500 – stock L 4,900. Campbell and Hunter Saddlers goods removed – no insurance. T. D. Harris Hardware total loss, the building believed to have been fireproof, insurance on building L 1,500 ditto on stock L1,100. Cheney & Co insurance L2,150: Stock and valuable furniture entirely destroyed. Thomas Hayes, Hardware stock mostly destroyed, insurance L800.

Mr. P Hanes (sp?) Groceries &c. good mostly destroyed – insurance £1,800. Thomas Thomson Mammoth House, large stock of dry goods destroyed. Insurance on buildings £1,100 – Heavy loss. Walker & Hutchison –

goods saved. T. Glassco (sp?) – insured £?50 – loss covered. Sabine & Higgins – insurance £450 - will cover loss. M. O'Donohue insured £1,700. **Patriot** office, Messrs' Kow?ell & Thomson insured £1,100. William Hall, dry goods, burnt our few months ago insured £750 stock partly saved. Foy & Austin insured on stock £1,500. Gary & Brown insured £650 – will cover loss. Mead & Co. – insured £900. R. C. Gwatkin, agent and Convey's hotel – no insurance. Mr. Brookes, Solicitor – books and papers saved – £1500 insured on the house belonging to Mr. Brookes, sen. Post's Hotel in Nelson Street – insurance £625. Duke street – Savings Bank – books and papers saved. In the North West side of Nelson Street - Charles Robertson – **Mirror** Office, all lost – insurance £250. Samuel Platt Tavern keeper – insurance on house and stock £1125 – loss £300 above. Mr. Crapper's Foundry – all lost but tools – building insured £400. H. MacNiven – dry goods stock insured for £100, furniture and stock entirely consumed. Wm. Henderson – dwelling house – insurance £100. John Naismith baker, furniture saved – insurance £400. Francis Street (East /Side) – contained several offices, shops and small houses, including Messrs, McLean & Jones chambers, R. Northcote's shop, Swaine & Co.'s medicine shop, Platt's stables &c. On the west side were Mr. Northcote's dwelling house, Bell & Lemon's tavern, several empty houses &c.

It is here chiefly that the loss will fall very severely, as several have lost all their furniture without being covered by insurance.

On the south side of King Street, some injury was done to the house occupied by Mr. Rogers, and that occupied by Mr. O'Beirne and belonging to the family of the late Mr. Badenach. The injury, however, was not material.

The heaviest loss on that side was sustained on the property in City Buildings.

The loss on the City Hall is estimated at £3,000; insurance on Walter McFarlane's stock in the City Hall is estimated at £1000; building and stock seriously injured, but the £1750 of insurance will more than cover the loss. We are happy to say that his large store in the opposite corner with its valuable escaped danger.

The following estimate has been made of the losses covered by insurance by the offices and may be relied upon:

CANADIAN OFFICES

B.N. American, Toronto	£17,000
Mutual Insurance	4,575
Montreal	2,500

BRITISH OFFICES

Alliance, London	£8150	
Globe "	2,050	
Phoenix "	4,100 – 14,600	

UNITED STATES OFFICES

Camden	£ 400
Hartford	3,900
Protection	1,350
Etna	3,600
Columbus	5,310 – 14,560
Total	£56,185

The next question is as to the total loss incurred by their calamity. Various were the conjectures on Saturday morning. By none was it estimated below £100,000, and a few below £150,000 and some run it up as high as £250,000 and £300,000. Our estimate then was that it was at least £100,000. We find *The Colonist* takes the same view, and we are now included to believe that the loss is below £100,000 rather than above it. One of the best judges of property in the city, estimates it at £80,000, which seems rather below the mark. It will be seen that more than the half is covered with insurance, which must materially lighten the burden of the sufferers, but there are still many who will be seriously injured by this fire3 and a large part of the insurance money must be paid by the residents of the city.

In whatever light the serious event be regarded, it must be acknowledged as a heavy blow and sore discouragement to Toronto, the heaviest it has received. There cannot be a doubt, however, that the activity and enterprise of the inhabitants will soon surmount the loss. The season is favourable for building and many improvements will doubtless be introduced in the formation of the new streets. Meantime there is a first duty to be looked to. We mean the relief of those who are o reduced by the fire as to require public assistance. There are causes of this kind, here a small assistance timely administered will revive the energies and raise the drooping spirits of those who may be ready to sink under the burden. We hope the public will not lose sight of this but come forward with a liberal hand when it is required. We send the assistance to distant places when it is needed and most surely not forget our own fellow citizens.

DISTRESSING DEATH OF MR. RICHARD WATSON BY THE FIRE

In the first account of this calamitous event, while mourning over its great extent and fearful consequences, there appeared one consolation, and that was a great one, viz. that no life had been lost. We lament to say that even that consolation we have been deprived of, by the death of a much-respected citizen. Mr. Watson, late publisher of the Canadian and of the Upper Canada Gazette lost his life in the performance of a friendly act to the proprietors of the Patriot office. Anxious to save some of the types which no one but a practical printer can properly handle, he rushed up the stairs to the highest storey of the office and remained too long, the floor having given way with him. One young man who was actively engaged in the same occupation, called to Mr. Watson that it was time to go: but he replied – it was time enough yet. this is the last which was heard of him in this life. For some time he was not missed as it was believed he had made his escape from the flames. But his not returning to his family early in the forenoon created alarm: The circumstances were inquired into and the worst was apprehended. His distracted wife could not be restrained from flying about the city inquiring for her lost husband. A cruel report reached her, that overcome with fatigue, Mr. Watson had taken shelter in a house and was asleep. This was traced to its foundation and found to be untrue. Engines were played on the burning ruins of the ***Patriot*** office and at length in the afternoon were found the remains of this unfortunate gentleman so mutilated as not to be recognized. The death of Mr. Watson is a subject of universal regret and it has this distressing aggravation that he leaves a widow and family entirely un-provided for. The Journal which he was connected was not a prosperous one and the ***Upper Canada Gazette*** was about to be abolished.

From a Parliamentary document lately published, it appeared that when Mr. Watson was appointed printer of the ***Gazette***, at the request of Mr. Stanton, in the year 1844, it was expressly stipulated that no compensation should be given him if the Government found it necessary to discontinue the Gazette or withdraw its emoluments. This we believe was a just and wise regulation, although we cannot help wishing that it had been otherwise, from the state of destitution of Mr. Watson's family. For twenty years Mr. Watson had the management as principal and confidential foreman in the Government office of the Upper Canada Gazette and for five years on his own account. We are aware of the danger of a pension list, for if not strictly watched, it has a constant tendency to exceed all due limits. And yet who would not plead, if it be consistent at all with the duty which the Government owes to the country, that something should be done for this bereave widow and family? There is a pension list in both Provinces amounting to between £4,000 and £5,000 per annum. By what regulations this is controlled we know not. But if the Government can do nothing, let the public take up the case and let t5he printing offices take the lead. It is not every day we have a man risking and losing his life from native kindness of heart and regard to his neighbour's interest, and the opportunity of marking it with a public testimonial in behalf of the sufferers by his loss, should not be left unimproved.

POSTSCRIPT

This is a work of fiction based on a real person and some real events. As I worked on the family genealogy, this man cried out to me as someone with whom I could relate. He lived in exciting times; he lived an adventurous life for a tradesman. And when he died, the reporter of the day wrote in the Globe Newspaper of Wednesday, April 11, 1849. 'Mr. Watson, late publisher of *The Canadian* and of the *Upper Canada Gazette* lost his life in the performance of a friendly act to the proprietors of the *Patriot* office.' To have that as an obituary was an inspiring tribute. To me, it deserved to be given a background. What inspires anyone to do that? What character qualities did he have to show that service in his final moments? I set about finding all the facts I could about the man and his times and that led to this work.

Where I could not find facts, I made them up – but consistent with what I knew. If others read this, I'm sure someone might be entertained by adding up both types. Should I worry that someday, readers might not be able to distinguish the fictions from the facts? Fortunately, there is not a single surviving copy of ***The Canadian*** I could find so I could make it what I wanted, or what I imagined Richard made it to be considering his other qualities. The names of the people Richard came across in this story are a blend of the fictitious and the factual.

Richard Watson was my actual Great Great Grandparent. He really was the third of that name in the family. It was because three generations of Richard's family had all been in the construction business and he never was that inspired me to wonder what had happened that Richard III was not a builder. I am pretty confident that he was not as big and brawny as those before him. If he was small or skinny, maybe it was because his mother was also. But his mother came from a family in the book business. I know that, which meant that she probably insisted that R III had to become educated. I made up what I think is a plausible scenario.

Richard III did marry Maryanne (or Maryanne or Mary Anne) Hopkins. Dates and names related to their marriage and children are a matter of written records of the time in St. John's Church, Limerick, Ireland and St. James Cathedral archives in Toronto Ontario. John, their first-borne, was born and christened in Limerick but never appeared in Toronto. I made up how he might have died even though it was painful for me to do so.

Andrew Watson was part owner of the ***Limerick***

Chronicle at the time Richard would have been an apprentice in the printing trade. Because Richard stepped into a job in Toronto almost right off the boat, I believe that Richard trained in the newspaper business rather than the book-printing business where his mother's father worked.

In my story, Richard and Maryanne come to Canada together. It didn't happen. Among the thousands of names of immigrants who travelled from Quebec to Montreal 1822-24, I found the name of 'Watson' ten times. Of the ten, there was only one 'Richard Watson'. He is listed as steerage passenger #133 aboard the **Car of Commerce**'s 13th trip up the river from Quebec to Montreal, leaving Quebec July 27, 1822. For that portion of his trip from Limerick to York (Toronto), he paid 10 shillings. It was a common practice for the husband to come alone, get a place and job, and then call for the family to join him. I could not find Maryanne 's name in a passenger register, but there were several collections of unnamed immigrants with whom she might have come, likely in 1823 (because Richard and Maryanne and a daughter (Sarah) in 1824). For artistic reasons, I had them come together.

William Lyon Mackenzie lived in Toronto at the time and Richard would have known him because of their shared vocation. John Lumsden was the name of a real man who worked in Mackenzie's shop. Robert Stanton and Charles Fothergill were actual previous owners of the ***Upper Canada Gazette***. Thomas Carfrae was the Grand Master of the St. Andrew's Masonic Lodge where Richard's name can be found as a member. Richard worked on a committee with Walter Rose. Sarah Watson, Richard's first child in Canada did marry Henry Price but I made up their earlier childhoods.

Anna Helena Watson, Richard's second daughter, did marry John Tully, brother of Kivas Tully who was a fellow member of the same Masonic Lodge as Richard. Why, among their five boys, Richard's name never appeared, is a cause of speculation. Here was a family with tradition up the yahoo and the pattern of their culture and family seems to be ignored. Two other dates cry out for explanation in that context. Why did Anna Helena wait so long to marry John Tully knowing she was pregnant? Who was making the decisions? I tried to make up a possible scenario. If you don't like it, feel free to make up your own!

John Harvey Watson, my Great Grandfather, and subject of the portrait, photograph and hand-written marriage certificate dated 1868, did go to Upper Canada College, I believe. There are two J. Watsons, one registered in 1841 and another in 1843. The parent of the first 'J. Watson' is identified as 'Mr. Watson'. How inconsiderate of the scribe over 150 years ago not to include an initial! But Richard was trying to join the upper class. He had the job held by a previous member of the Family Compact. I'll bet he used all other avenues to accomplish that elevation i.e. sending his son to the place where the aristocracy sent their sons, marrying his daughter to a lawyer (who later became a judge), and doing favours for those further up the social ladder he sought to climb. I think when it came to climbing that ladder, or helping his countrymen, I think he chose his people – at least that is the way I wrote the story.

Richard Watson's name appears in a database of Criminals listed as being in Toronto and District Jail in 1837. At the time, there were two other 'Richard Watsons' in the Census of Toronto, but ours was the only one till then. The other two are a father and son, one a carpenter and the other a tinsmith. If you don't like my scenario about how it happened Richard was in jail, here is another chance to be creative. I think my story was a real possibility because the Wanted Poster for William Lyon Mackenzie that Richard either composed, set in type or proofread, is actually date stamped at 3 PM. To get that out, Richard worked late. And if he was found on the street with ink on his hands, he might well have been seen as a traitorous friend of the most-wanted printer in the poster.

Sophia Dalton took over ownership of the *Patriot* newspaper for almost 10 years after her husband died. She was Toronto's first successful female publisher.

About the same time, Amelia Bloomer started a newspaper exclusively targeted at women in New York 1n 1849. It didn't happen without earlier interest and perhaps effort. So Maryanne could have been in the vanguard of the suffragette movement when I placed her as a contributor to a newspaper. Sophia sold the newspaper to Edward O'Brien in Oct 1848, mere months before the fire. I wonder if that was a contributing factor to Richard's being in that building at all – misplaced chivalry! Robert Crockett was an actual sergeant in the Militia, but in the Hamilton Company where John Harvey Watson served in 1868. Joe Weedrick. He really was a fisherman (if I have his name spelled correctly) in the 1940's, not the 1840's

All the rest of the names are made up, some by my grandchildren.

It has always been a mystery to me why Richard was downtown at 2 AM when the fire broke out. Why wasn't he at home in bed? So I made up a reason. It really was the Easter Weekend.

The penknife? I made that up because I did blacksmithing at one time and it would have been a great idea before spring-backed blades became widespread.

I find myself at odds with the work of some other current writers of this period. They tend to focus on the arrogance and abusive and especially the violence that was undoubtedly part of life then. I chose not to, as much as I could. I strongly believe there is an unwritten history that has passed orally for a long time. In those days, I think one's ancestry was known by neighbours for generations, as you knew theirs. This knowledge could soften judgments. I suspect that women had long ago figured out the benefits of assistance to each other if the men hadn't. In the midst of the most awful of times, compassion and caring events pop up. They are treated as aberrations. I don't think they were as rare as we make out, and that women were most likely the custodians of such sharing care. What makes them seem rare could be explained by the fact that the men wrote the history we read. The women carry the history we hear if we chose.

A reader of this work could be very critical – too Polyanna-ish, delusional, trite – apart from an ignorance of paragraphing protocols. I can imagine them all. But I believe people are, or in unguarded moments can be, better than they are portrayed or think themselves to be. So if this narrative seems too cartoonish – too bad!

I imagine someone summarizing this effort, if they are being charitable, as a 'nice outline'. One critic complained I did not describe enough of the clothing. I agree I might have described more details, including clothing, more smells, more thoughts, more…. and then whose story would it be? Another factor in the shortening exercise was the fact that more research and a longer text would have taken longer and made me ask if I was prepared to invest more and more time in the project for minimal, if any, return. Would it be better by a dozen more drafts? If you'd like to find out, go ahead.

Others who read early drafts were flattering. They 'liked' the vignettes. Good! This effort was written to entertain me and any other imaginative reader and memorialize a pioneer in whose lineage I stand. I never intended to compete for a Giller Prize. If your summary of the time spent reading this tale was that it was wasted, I'm sorry! If your imagination was tickled to believe my ancestry and everyone else's was as spicy, civil, and skilled as I think they were, then we both spent our time well.

Poetry

From Penny's Poetry pages wiki in: Articles using Wikipedia text, Imported, updated, or created in 2011, Stanzaic form, and 2 more The idiosyncratic link between spelling and pronunciation in the English language is explored in this Scottish example (the name Menzies is pronounced 11px /ˈmɪŋɪs/ ming-iss).

'A lively young damsel named Menzies Inquired: "Do you know what this thenzies?"   Her aunt, with a gasp, Replied: "It's a wasp, And you're holding the end where the stenzies".' The earliest known use of the name "Limerick" for the form is an 1880 reference, in a Saint John, New Brunswick newspaper, to an apparently well-known tune "Won't you Come to Limerick."
Apparently, the limerick could be sung to that tune.

There was a young rustic named Mallory,
who drew but a very small salary.
When he went to the show,
his purse made him go
to a seat in the uppermost gallery.

Alternates

There was an Old Man of Nantucket
Who kept all his cash in a bucket.
His daughter, called Nan,
Ran away with a man,
And as for the bucket, Nantucket.
- Anonymous

Limerick: There was an Old Man with a Beard
No. 1 from *A Book of Nonsense* (1846) and included in
'Two hundred years of nonsense' by Edward Lear

'There was an old man with a beard
Who said, "it's just how I feared!
Two owls and a hen
Four larks and a wren
Have all built their nests in my beard.'

www.ingramcontent.com/pod-product-compliance
Lightning Source LLC
Chambersburg PA
CBHW020358030726
47496CB00007B/2196